# The
# Serpent's
# Spell

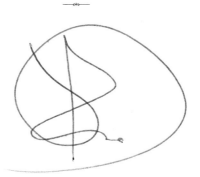

# The
# Serpent's
# Spell

RAE BRIDGMAN

GREAT PLAINS
PUBLICATIONS

Great Plains Publications
420 – 70 Arthur Street
Winnipeg, MB  R3B 1G7
www.greatplains.mb.ca

Great Plains Publications gratefully acknowledges the financial support provided for its publishing program by the Government of Canada through the Book Publishing Industry Development Program (BPIDP); the Canada Council for the Arts; as well as the Manitoba Department of Culture, Heritage and Tourism; and the Manitoba Arts Council.

Design & Typography by Relish Design Studios Ltd.
Printed in Canada by Friesens

**CANADIAN CATALOGUING IN PUBLICATION DATA**

Main entry under title:

Bridgman, Rae
    The serpent's spell / Rae Bridgman.

    ISBN 1-894283-67-8

    I. Title

PS8603.R528S47  2006    jC813'.6    C2006-900499-4

Middle Gate

Trunion Square

East Field

West Field

Gruffud's Academy

*For My Children*
*and My Children's Children...*

*Where is the gate to MiddleGate?*

## *Where do all the snakes come from?*

*Qui legitis flores et humi nascentia fraga,*
*frigidus, o pueri (fugite hinc!), latet anguis in herba.*

Children, all of you plucking flowers and strawberries,
A cold snake—flee from here!
A cold snake lurks in the grass.

—From Virgil's *Eclogues* III.92–93.

*ANGUIS* (the Snake, but also the star *Draco*) is the origin of all serpents, because they can be folded and bent, and hence snakes are called anguis since they are angular and never straight.

*COLUBER* (another name for snake) is called this because *colat umbras*—it inhabits shady places—or else because it glides with serpentine coils (*colubrosus*) into slippery courses. It is known as the "slippery one" because it slips away crawling, and, like a fish, the more so the tighter it is held.

*SERPENS* gets it name because it creeps (*serpit*) by secret approaches and not by open steps. It moves along by very small pressures of its scales....

Of these creatures, how many poisons there are, how many species, how many calamities, how many griefs, and what a lot of different colours they have!

—From T.H. White's *The Bestiary: A Book of Beasts, Being a Translation from a Latin Bestiary of the Twelfth Century.*

# Contents

# Prologue

*Life is short, but books never die.*

---

*NIGRO LAPILLO NOTARE DIEM.*

**MARK THE DAY WITH A BLACK STONE.**

---

" ...Roger Sterling with Toronto's own CQOY 99.9 on this muggy August day—a real scorcher.

"Stay tuned for an interview with Silas Royal, lead singer with Shadows!

"And this just in from our CQOY local news service...

"Firefighters were called to a blaze on Harbinger Street in Toronto this morning. The fire threatened an entire city block of three-storey brick row houses. Dead is Hazel Wychwood, seventy-one years old. She is survived by her ten-year-old grandson, William.

"Inspector Jack Findstein reported, 'It's arson, but we don't know why yet.'

"Blue Sky Bakery, the White Lotus Chinese Restaurant and Imperial Boots all suffered extensive smoke damage. Pirsstle and Bertram's Antiquarian Booksellers shop was spared. We'll have more details for you on CQOY's 12 o'clock newscast.

"Who said books can't be killed by fire? *Liber longus, vita brevis.* Life is short, but books never die. Any of our listeners know where that quote comes from?

"Give us a shout at CQOY 99.9—caller number 9 wins tickets to Friday's Shadows concert..."

# 1 The Night Before

*What is the stuff of fears and dreams?*

---

*VIVERE EST PINGERE.*
TO LIVE IS TO DOODLE.

---

The candle spluttered in the half-dark, and Sophie's shadow wavered against the bedroom wall. Sitting at her desk, she stared down at a page filled with row after row of letters scrawled in green ink. By the flickering candlelight her eyeglass frames turned from bright orange to murky green. She turned the page over, picked up her pen, dipped it in the bottle of green ink on the desk and then drew a large letter *S* decorated with winged cats and bees with long stingers.

Curled up on Sophie's bed was a white cat with a black diamond face and striped tail. Every time the pen scratched against the paper, its whiskers twitched and its golden eyes blinked.

The pen scratched once more, and the ink...b-l-o-t-t-e-d.

Sophie grimaced, scrunched up the paper and threw it onto the floor.

The cat pounced on the ball of paper and batted it about for a moment, then jumped up onto Sophie's lap.

"Oh, Cadmus, you almost made me spill the ink."

Sophie scratched the cat's ears for a moment, then pulled out another sheet of paper and dipped the pen in the bottle again. This time, she scrawled the word *WILLIAM*, adding porcupine prickles and cat claws to the *W* and a thick, bare rat's tail to the *M*.

Staccato footsteps mounted the stairs—Aunt Rue's footsteps.

"Sophie, you're not still drawing, are you?" asked Aunt Rue in an exasperated tone. "It's long past your bedtime. You know we've got a big day tomorrow with your cousin William coming."

"No...I mean yes, Aunt Rue," Sophie called. She pushed the cat off her lap. "I'm in bed—snoring."

The cat settled back at the foot of the bed and began to wash its whiskers.

Sophie closed the lid of the bottle and wiped the pen clean. With a last look at the needle-like prickles she had drawn, she smiled.

Then she blew out the candle, jumped into bed and pulled up her rumpled covers.

# 11 Night Train

*Why does it bite its own tail?*

---

*TE IPSUM ABSCONDE ET QUAERE.*

HIDE AND GO SEEK.

---

Clutching a cage to his chest, Wil stood by the train and gazed down its glistening, steel-plated length. A whoosh of compressed air from under the train made him jump.

"Mind the steps, son," said the porter, whose skin was green under the fluorescent lights. "Why don't I take that birdie cage for you?"

"No, thank you," said Wil. "It's not a—"

But the porter was already looking away.

A speaker overhead crackled. "All passengers, Toronto to Winnipeg, departing from Gate 9 at six o'clock. Last call for Gate 9 to Winnipeg."

Wil mounted the steps and turned to wave to Mr. Bertram, but he couldn't find Mr. Bertram's grey hat in the crowd. Wil felt a lump in his throat, and stumbled up the remaining steps into the coach. He teetered down the narrow aisle past a man with thick eyeglasses who was reading a fat book with the title *Imaginary Places.*

Wil tried to squeeze past a mother busy settling twin boys, who were both wearing striped yellow and black shirts. They reminded Wil of plump bumblebees.

"Excuse me, please," he said.

Startled, the mother looked up at Wil. "Sorry," she said. Turning back to the twins, she scolded them both. "Roger, turn around, pumpkin, and Kirby, sweetie, please sit down—now."

Wil approached the last remaining seat. An elderly woman wearing a dress with large purple flowers was sitting opposite. Her hair—as dark purple as grape jelly—was pulled up high in a bun, which was leaning dangerously to one side.

Wil sat down with the cage on his lap and watched the purple woman as she tried to squeeze a box under her seat. Then he peered out the window. There was Mr. Bertram waving his hat right beneath Wil's window. He bowed to Wil and tipped his hat once before disappearing into the throng.

Wil settled back into his seat, already missing Mr. Bertram and the green peppermints he always carried in his pocket. Mr. Bertram had lots of proverbs—not that Wil always understood what they meant.

"Dying is another chapter in the book of life, my boy," Mr. Bertram had told him.

"But if life is like a book, why can't you turn back the pages?" Wil had asked. "Or skip ahead? Why not rip out the parts you don't want to read?" But Mr. Bertram had looked shocked at the very idea of ripping pages from a book.

Wil turned back to the purple woman, who was now muttering to herself.

"You have to fit. No other spot for you." When she had stuffed the box under her seat, she sat up and looked at Wil.

"Hello, my dear," she said, panting. "Are you travelling to Winnipeg?"

"Yes," said Wil in a small voice.

"A long trip for you to be making all by yourself, isn't it—all the way from Toronto to Winnipeg?"

"Yes," said Wil, with a hint of defiance in his voice this time.

"And how old are you, my dear?"

"I'm nine," said Wil. "I mean, I'm ten. I just had my birthday," he blurted.

"Good for you." The purple woman beamed at him, and began to rummage in her purse. "Where did you go?" she crooned. "I know you're in here somewhere."

Does she always talk to things? Wil wondered.

"Got you!" she exclaimed. "You can't escape me!" With a look of triumph, she donned a pair of pointy, purple-rimmed eyeglasses.

"What's in your cage, my dear? Why...it's a snake!"

The twins, who had escaped their mother, trundled towards Wil. One pointed at the cage. "Nake, nake, nake?"

"Yes, this is Esme," said Wil. "Want to see her?"

The children's heads bobbed up and down, and Wil opened the cage. He cupped Esme in his hand, and the children reached out to touch her.

At the same moment, the mother yanked the children away. "A snake!" she screamed.

Wil was so startled that he dropped Esme, who slithered under the purple woman's seat.

The twins crawled after Esme. "Hide-and-go-seek, hide-and-go-seek," they chanted.

Before Wil could see where Esme had gone, a man several seats away dove to the floor. In a daze, Wil noticed the man had a cane with a carved head—the head of a snake with glittering ruby eyes. It looks almost alive, he thought.

The man poked the cane under the seats. "I know you're in there," he said. He must have poked one of the twins. Roger or Kirby—Wil couldn't tell which—began to bawl.

Another man, ashen-faced, perched on top of his seat and waved a white handkerchief, as if surrendering.

A woman rolled up her newspaper in a determined fashion. "Don't worry, I'll get it," she called down the aisle.

It seemed Esme had no intention of being captured, however. Wil caught sight of her slithering towards the other end of the car. He tried to clamber past the man with the cane and the woman with the newspaper, but the way was blocked.

"Help! I've been bitten!" someone shrieked.

A flurry of voices broke out. "It's here." "No, it's over here." "There it is. No, no, not there—over here!"

"Esme can't bite," Wil shouted, trying to make himself heard. "Esme won't hurt anyone. She's not poisonous, I mean, she's not venomous!"

But no one listened.

"What's going on? *Qu'est-ce qui se passe ici?*" said a deep voice from behind Wil.

Wil turned and looked up into the puffy face of the conductor, whose pencil-line moustache was twitching.

"My snake escaped—

"—your what?"

"My—my snake, sir." Wil cleared his throat, but his voice only quavered more. "She can't bite anyone—she's not that kind of snake. She hasn't even got fangs." Wil felt hot tears well up.

"Well, where has it got to?" asked the conductor, his eyes scanning the coach, as he drew a pair of spotless white gloves from his pocket. "It can't have gone too far."

Making his way past the man with the white handkerchief, who was still standing on his seat, the conductor bent down and nabbed the squirming Esme.

"Is this it?" he asked Wil and he held Esme out like a dirty sock.

Esme twisted from side to side. Her forked tongue darted in the air.

"Yes—yes, sir," Wil said.

"Good. We'll put it back in its cage," said the conductor, speaking as if Wil were dim-witted. "I'll take the cage to the animal compartment, shall I? Where it belongs," he added as he opened the lid to plop Esme inside. "Now, I suggest you return to your seat."

Wil nodded, feeling miserable.

Roger and Kirby, the twin bumblebees, were snivelling.

Their mother marched them back to their seats. "Snakes are bad—never touch snakes. Nasty, dirty things. They bite...and you can die!"

"Diiiii—eeeee. Diiiii—eeeee. Diiiii—eeeee," Roger and Kirby repeated after their mother.

Wil tried to ignore the babble of complaints around him—wishing he weren't on this train...wishing he were back home again...wishing nothing had happened.

The lights flickered and the train finally pulled out of the station. It dragged past the hotel with the green roof, past the market, past the old factories, past the sailboats in the harbour, past the white bridge, past tall apartment buildings and more houses than Wil could count. Gaining speed, it left the city and twisted along the shimmering lake...until the city was left far behind.

Trees...trees...and more trees. The sky turned a deep crimson over the rolling hills, and Wil could hear the long drawn-out wail of the train rounding the curve of the lake—"For-r-r-r-r-r-r-r-ev-er."

———✺———

The train was quiet now, but for the melancholy strains of a song leaking from a radio somewhere—*O home, far, far away, why don't you take me home, sweet home...*

Wil pulled out the supper Mr. Bertram had packed for him from his pocket. The honey sandwiches were soggy, but he was hungry. He gazed out the darkening window, and saw his own reflection. A wan, freckled face stared back at him. Black almond-shaped eyes were almost hidden by a shock of brown hair. One of the dark night clouds circled around the reflection in the window; the head of the cloud looked like it was about to bite its tail.

Wil shivered and turned away.

# III  The Black Medallion

*Wil fumbled in his pocket and pulled out a small metal pouch.*

---
*MUNUS ET ONUS.*

A GIFT AND A BURDEN.

---

In vain, Wil tried to sleep; he tossed and turned, but only succeeded in getting a crick in his neck. With the dimming of the lights, the rhythmic chugging of the train had rocked almost everyone else to sleep. Heads lolled and bodies slumped. The purple woman was snoring. Even the twins were fast asleep after pestering their mother to see "nake" again.

Wil fumbled in his pocket and pulled out a small metal pouch. He opened its rusty clasp and drew out a black medallion and gold ring, remembering the night they had been given to him.

It was his birthday, and Gran had made a pot of his favourite stew. Even now, his mouth watered at the thought of it. After supper, Gran had brought out a package wrapped in brown paper and string.

"William, it's time for you to have these; they belonged to your parents," she had said, her voice shaking a little, and her blue eyes—magnified by her eyeglasses—glistened as if she were about to cry.

Wil's eyes had widened, for his grandmother hardly ever mentioned his mother and father. He opened the package to find a small pouch.

Gran watched him and her gnarled hands fidgeted.

He opened the clasp to the pouch. Its pink silk lining was frayed; inside, he found the black medallion and gold ring. He cradled them in his hand.

"Gran...they're amazing. Thank you."

The gold ring was worn and scratched. Wil slipped it off the chain and tried it on his middle finger, but it was much too big—too big even for his thumb.

The black medallion was a coin-sized disc hanging from a crescent moon. On one side of the disc, the tiny gold symbol of a snake shimmered on the dull black surface, surrounded by the outline of a silver arrow. On the other side of the medallion, the simple outline of a silver triangle glimmered.

"What does the snake mean, Gran?"

She smiled, her lips trembling. "Imagine, ten years old already! You are a young man now. Never let these out of your sight. Always keep them with you."

"Why?" asked Wil.

His grandmother's lips had tightened.

———

"What am I supposed to do?" murmured Wil to himself. "Carry this medallion and ring around with me for the rest of my life?"

Perhaps they're valuable, he thought.

But if they're that valuable, someone else might want them—and want them badly enough to kill me.

I'm being paranoid. Just because Gran—

Look, they were a birthday present. She didn't want to put me in any danger.

But maybe she didn't know.

Wil was startled from these thoughts by the train whistle blowing. They were passing through another small town. Still holding the medallion and the ring, he groped for the letter in his pocket. and heard the reassuring crinkle of paper.

"Well, how are you feeling, my dear—hmmm?" a sleepy voice murmured.

Wil looked up into bleary, green eyes behind purple-rimmed eyeglasses. He quickly stuffed the medallion and ring back into the pouch.

Before he could answer, the purple woman was asleep again. Her mouth was agape, and Wil noticed a piece of lettuce stuck in her teeth. He looked away, still holding the small pouch tight to his chest.

# IV  An Awful Discovery

*Snake's tongue!*

---

*FABULA INVOLUTA EST.*
THE PLOT THICKENS.

---

Sophie sat at the kitchen table prodding breadcrumbs into a spiral. Her eyeglass frames were pale yellow, matching a half-hearted sun poking above the treetops. With a high-pitched whistle, *The Daily Magezine* shot down the chimney and spewed ashes. Sophie unfurled it and her eyeglass frames turned crimson red.

"Look!" she exclaimed.

"What is it?" asked Aunt Rue, as she shuffled through a stack of reports.

"Not good," said Sophie, her head buried in the paper.

"What's happened?" asked Aunt Rue sharply.

"There's a picture here of hundreds of snakes slithering across rocks."

WHO IS KILLING MANITOBA'S GARTER SNAKES?
GRIM DISCOVERY SPARKS ANGER

"Snake's tongue!" exclaimed Aunt Rue, her voice rising.

*Hundreds of snake corpses in fields surrounding the Narcisse caves northwest of Winnipeg have sparked revulsion and anger at what appears to be calculated serpicide.*

*"I got this horrible feeling I'd walked into a grisly crime scene right out of a movie," said Isadora Coop, who discovered the dead snakes while walking her dogs Maggie and Erasmus.*

*The grim discovery sparked disgust and started speculation about possible culprits. No group has yet claimed responsibility for the atrocity. Rodney Clapton, Executive Director of A.D.D.E.R. (Association for the Destruction and Disposal of Evil Reptiles) denied responsibility. "Everyone knows the snakes of Narcisse are harmless," he said. Representatives of the North American and European chapters of I.S.N.O.G.—*

"Pronounced eye-snog, dear. Quite a disreputable organization," said Aunt Rue, her voice sounding strained.

Sophie continued to read:

*—(International Snakes No! Guild) could not be reached. Authorities have no concrete leads about the culprit.*

*A government official, who spoke anonymously, has confirmed hundreds of snakes were found dead one year ago; the matter was not made public. The Order of the Snakes has demanded a full inquiry into why no action was taken.*

*The snakes are returning to their caves before the first frost, and further attacks are feared. [Report by Reece Rebus]*

"What about the field trip to the snakepits this year?" asked Sophie, nibbling at her thumbnail.

"Don't bite your nails, dear," said Aunt Rue and she crammed all the reports into her bag. "This must be why there's an emergency meeting of all departments this afternoon."

# V The Letter

*What if there hadn't been a fire that day?*

---

*NOLI STARE IN SEDILI LATRINAE.*

BEST NOT TO STAND ON A TOILET SEAT.

---

The black sky turned drizzle-grey. Six more hours until Winnipeg. Wil closed his eyes, but every time he closed them, he saw flames licking blackened bricks.

Was it only one week ago?

He had woken up early that Saturday morning. Esme was coiled inside her hut, her scales gently expanding and contracting with each breath. On his way to the kitchen, he checked his grandmother. One of her blankets had slipped to the floor. When he pulled it over her, she did not stir. After scribbling a note about warm bagels from the bakery, he crept down the stairs. But the third stair from the bottom squeaked, and he remembered he was supposed to take Esme to the bookstore.

He scaled the stairs to find Esme still in her hut. Just one eye, a shiny snout and the tiny line of her mouth were visible.

"We're going to Pirsstle and Bertram's today, Esme."

Esme flicked her tongue towards Wil, as if she understood.

Balancing Esme's cage, Wil teetered down the stairs and opened the door to the street. He felt a steamy blast of hot, humid air. Harbinger

Street was empty but for a single jogger. Wil turned a few paces left and slipped inside the bookstore to the jangle of a brass bell. Mr. Bertram was already helping a customer.

Ever since Wil could remember, he had spent all his spare time in the bookstore. The gold-lettered sign out front read:

*Pirsstle and Bertram's*
ANTIQUARIAN BOOKSELLERS
*Specializing in Rare Books & Manuscript Restoration*

Even though Mr. Pirsstle had died many years ago, Mr. Bertram always said it would insult Mr. Pirsstle's memory to change the name.

Inside was a maze of overflowing, rickety shelves—with antique leather-bound books alongside family Bibles, maps and atlases, dictionaries, novels, comics, children's nursery rhymes and picture books, mysteries, scientific treatises, plays and poetry. There was even a collection of miniature books under lock and key. If there were some hidden order to the collection, Wil had never discovered it. Mr. Bertram, though, seemed to have an uncanny sense of where each book was, and no one ever left the store empty-handed.

Wil set Esme's cage down on the wooden counter just as the brass bell rang again, and a man with ruddy cheeks and double chins stepped into the shop. The man smoothed down his thin hair, which looked as if it had been dyed with black shoe polish.

"My first visit to your establishment," said the man in a wheezy voice. "Been meaning to come here for years."

"We're the best bookstore in the country," Wil had said proudly.

"Yes, so I've heard," said the man, smiling. "I'll just look around a bit, if you don't mind."

With a quick wave to Mr. Bertram, Wil had slipped out of the shop and hurried over to Harbord Bakery. And that was when everything had changed.

Forever...

...Wil looked out the train window and watched lights from a small town flicker by and then vanish. He closed his eyes and tried to fall asleep one last time, but now all he could think about was roiling, choking yellow smoke, fire trucks and fat hoses slithering along the street.

Rivulets of water were running down the pavement. Alarms rang and sirens filled the air. As Wil had run home across Harbinger Street, his heart pounding in his chest, the paper bag he was carrying split open...and bagels spilled out and rolled across the pavement.

"Hey, young fellow, get back to the other side," shouted a police officer.

"My grandmother's up there," shouted Wil, pointing to her window on the third floor, but the police officer was busy directing traffic.

Desperate, Wil ran and pulled at the arm of one of the firefighters. "My Gran is up there. Please, you've got to save her."

The man's eyes glinted from behind his visor. He grasped Wil's shoulder for a moment and headed toward the ladders.

Wil crossed back to the other side, kicking bagels out of his way. The smoke turned a dense charcoal and the morning sun turned sick-orange. With a huge crack, a stained-glass window on the second floor of Wil's building exploded, and great arcs of water shot out onto the street. The smoke billowed steamy white.

Unblinking, Wil had stared at the plant on the third-floor windowsill. If the plant's alive, Gran must be safe, Wil had promised himself...

The purple woman stirred in her sleep, and Wil was jarred from his thoughts once more. Gritty streaks of rain were spitting across his window. As far as his eyes could see—endless, flat, yellow fields. Wil felt something wet on his cheek and wiped it away. Inching his way down the aisle, he headed to the washroom and passed the twins, who were both awake, their faces sticky with red jam.

The washroom's OCCUPIED sign was glowing red. Wil paced back and forth in the aisle until at last the washroom door opened, and the man who had waved the white handkerchief slipped out.

There were signs posted everywhere in the tiny washroom. *Please Wash Hands With Soap. No Food Down Sink. No Smoking. Do Not Dispose of Children's Diapers in This Area.*

Wil flushed the toilet, which emptied with a frightening whoosh, and then pushed the knob on the soap container. A cold, green, antiseptic glob plopped into his palm. He grimaced and hurried to wash up. When he had finished, he tried to open the door, but it was locked.

Another tiny sign above the door handle read

*To Lock Door Turn Latch to Left.*
*To Unlock Door Turn Latch to Right.*

Wil turned the latch to the right and tried to open the door again.
It was jammed.
Wil kicked at the door.

"Can anyone hear me? I'm stuck. Anyone there?"

He put his ear to the door. All he could hear was the train's rhythmic chugging. Pounding at the door, he shouted, "Help!"

No one answered.

His eyes fell on another sign with an arrow pointing to a small red button.

*For Assistance, Press Emergency Button*

The emergency button was just above his reach, so he clambered on top of the toilet and pushed the button. But at that very moment, the train pitched to one side. Wil slipped...and struck his head against the door.

Someone knocked on the door. "Hello? Anyone in there? The emergency light's on out here."

"Help! I'm stuck," shouted Wil.

"Don't panic. We'll have you out in a jiffy," said a deep voice.

"Who's in there?" said a woman's voice. "Is someone stuck in there?"

"I've got to take a whiz—of all the luck," someone else said.

The door handle rattled, and Wil could feel someone pushing against the door.

"It's one of those newfangled designs—designed to trap people, if you ask me," said the deep voice.

Glumly, Wil rubbed his head as he read yet another sign hanging above the sink.

*Do Not Stand on Sink or Toilet.*

The clamour of voices outside the washroom grew. "Has anyone got a hammer?" "Well, there must be an emergency release catch here somewhere." "Why's the line so long, eh?"

"What's all this commotion?" said a voice that sounded as if it belonged to the purple woman.

"The door's jammed, ma'am," said the deep voice.

Not a moment later, Wil heard the door handle open smoothly.

Someone hoisted Wil out from the washroom

"Careful...there you go, son," said the man with the deep voice.

The purple woman took Wil by the hand, and led him back to his seat. "Time for some brunch, I think. What would you like?" Without even waiting for a reply, she bustled down the aisle.

With his head throbbing, Wil reached into his pocket and pulled out a crumpled letter.

**17**

*Dear William:*

*We are picking you up at the train station. Aunt Rue and Aunt Violet are glad you are coming. I hope you have a good train ride. I am ten years old too. We will be learning snapdragon this year.*

*Yours truly,*

*Sophie Isidor*

The letter ended with fancy spirals and curlicues around the *S* and the *I.*
Wil wondered for the umpteenth time what snapdragon was. A snapdragon was a small snapping flower, and according to nine different dictionaries at Pirsstle and Bertram's, it was also a game. A game of snatching raisins from burning brandy. But why would anyone want to play with fire? Only *The Lexicon of Extinct English Words*—filled with strange expressions no one used any more—said snapdragon was an ancient shadow game...whatever that meant.

Mr. Bertram had shaken his head when Wil asked him about snap-dragon. "That's a mouthful, Wil. Words are like the daughters of the moon, and dictionaries, like watches. The worst is better than none at all and the best is never quite true."

When Wil had said he didn't want to play any game of fire, Mr. Bertram had sighed and patted him on the shoulder.

Now here he was, going to live with two aunts and a cousin he didn't even know. His grandmother had never mentioned them—not even once. He had asked Mr. Bertram, "Why did Gran never tell me I had a family?" But Mr. Bertram had looked away and started talking about the weather, so Wil didn't try asking again.

Wil put the letter back into his pocket. His head was throbbing more than ever, as the purple woman reappeared with a triumphant smile.

"Eat up, my dear," she said.

At the sight of blueberry muffins and cinnamon buns drizzled with honey, a pool of brown sugar on hot oatmeal and three juicy strawberries on a slice of honeydew melon, the throbbing in Wil's head suddenly evaporated.

"Th-thank you," he stammered.

Not noticing other passengers had only burnt toast and lumpy cereal—and they were ogling his feast—Wil munched happily on the juicy strawberries.

# VI Train Station

*The train slid into the station.*

---

*QUOD SI?*

WHAT IF?

---

P orters pushed through the crowds beneath a grand glass dome in the train station, while Sophie and Aunt Rue stood at the base of a huge marble column. Everyone seemed to be hurrying to greet friends and relatives. Twins wearing black and yellow striped shirts—Sophie thought they looked like bees—giggled and ran to a tall bearded man, who must have been their father.

"Take my hand, dear," said Aunt Rue. "I don't want you getting lost."

Sophie held out her hand, hoping Aunt Rue wouldn't smudge the lizard drawing on her palm. Why does Aunt Rue think I'm going to get lost anyway, thought Sophie as she looked up at the departures and arrivals screen. Halifax, Montreal, Ottawa, Toronto ...

"Look, the train came in ten minutes ago, Aunt Rue," said Sophie. "What if I don't like him?" she added in a small voice.

"Yes, I know the train has arrived, dear," said Aunt Rue, sounding distracted as she looked in one direction then the other and gripped Sophie's hand more tightly. "But I don't see Aunt Violet anywhere. And where is your cousin William?"

# VII  Half Moon Lane

*How many years have they been staring at each other?*

*MURUS ET SPECULUM UNUM ET IDEM.*

*SPECIEI NE QUICQUAM CREDAS.*

IS A BRICK WALL NOT LIKE A MIRROR?

DO NOT TRUST APPEARANCES TOO MUCH.

Wil walked out of the train station with Esme's cage held tight to his chest. The hot noon sun and porters' shouting made him feel dizzy. What if no one came? As his eyes strained to find his two aunts and cousin—without having any idea what they looked like—he saw a man who seemed familiar. A uniformed chauffeur bowed to the man and opened the door to a long, grey limousine.

"Thank you, Gifford," said the man. "Any news?"

"Nothing yet, sir."

The man ran his hand through his thin black hair. "*Tempus fugit.* Time is of the essence," he said.

At the gesture, Wil recognized him. It was the same man who had visited Pirsstle and Bertram's the morning of the fire. He must be somebody important.

"Are you William Wychwood?" said a voice behind Wil.

Wil turned, his heart skipping a beat. A thin woman with a worn face and coiled, grey braids was holding the hand of a girl, who was wearing eyeglasses framed in red and white polka dots.

"Yes, I'm, I'm Wil...but with one *l*, not with two," Wil blurted out.

"I see," said the woman with a slightly strained smile. "Well, we're glad you're safe, Wil-with-one-*l*-not-with-two. I'm your Aunt Rue and this is your cousin Sophie. Now what about your luggage?"

"I've got everything—just Esme, my snake," Wil said.

Sophie peered into the cage with interest, while Wil stared at his aunt, trying to see if she looked like his mother.

According to Gran, both his parents had died in a car accident when he was a year old. He couldn't summon any memories of his parents and had only seen one photograph of them. They were standing on a beach and smiling as they looked towards the camera. His father was tall and thin, and his mother stood no taller than his shoulder. Her eyes were dark and almond-shaped, like Wil's own—and like Aunt Rue's.

"You've brought nothing else with you?" asked Aunt Rue, sounding puzzled.

"Everything...the fire—"

"Yes, yes, of course," said Aunt Rue briskly, as if she regretted asking the question. "We'll get more things for you," she said, patting him on the shoulder. "Would you like me to take Esme?"

"No—no, thank you."

"We're meeting Aunt Violet also," said Aunt Rue, glancing around. "She was coming on the same train. Perhaps—"

At the mention of her name, Aunt Violet hove into sight, waving her handkerchief. It was none other than the purple woman, who gave Sophie and Aunt Rue an affectionate peck on each cheek.

"Perhaps you and Wil met on the train already, Aunt Violet," said Aunt Rue.

As Aunt Violet's eyes focused on him, Wil felt his face turning crimson.

"Yes, we did share the train ride, didn't we? And a couple of small adventures besides," said Aunt Violet, her eyes twinkling. "I'm so sorry about your grandmother, my dear. Imagine we were sitting across from each other all this time and didn't even know we were proper family."

But Wil had a strange feeling that Aunt Violet had known all along.

"Let's go home," said Aunt Rue. "The bus is just across the street."

By the time they had crossed the street, the bus—bright peacock blue with *MIDDLEGATE BUS LINES TRAVEL UNLIMITED* in bold yellow and white letters—was practically filled.

"Sophie, why don't you sit on the other side of Aunt Violet, and Wil, there's room for you and Esme over there beside Mr. Oystein," said Aunt Rue, pointing to a vacant seat near the driver.

Mr. Oystein turned out to be the man with the snake's head cane. He was talking in a loud voice to the driver.

"...the funniest thing I've seen in a long time, Mr. Scrimshaw."

The driver snorted. "You know, that reminds me of the time I was working nearby those snakepits. I put my pants on one morning. They was hangin' over the back of the chair so they wouldn't wrinkle, you know. Well, I pulled them up right as rain, but soon discovered"—he almost doubled over as he chuckled—"I soon discovered, I was not alone. Talk about hoppin' with a snake up my pant leg!"

Mr. Oystein laughed until tears were streaming down his face.

Wil looked out the window, hardly seeing a thing. He did not think the story was very funny and wondered what happened to the snake.

The driver glanced in his rear view mirror. "Best be on our way then, since we're all loaded up."

The bus weaved along busy streets and as it stopped at a red light, Wil's eyes fixed on an ornate wrought-iron door decorated with two green serpents, which looked as though they were guarding the door. Then the bus jolted along a side street pitted with potholes until it turned into a large, deserted parking lot by a brick house. It seemed to be the only house in the area, surrounded as it was by a sea of parking lots dotted with warehouses. A rising sunburst decorated the peak of the house, and a five-pointed star graced each corner.

Why were they stopping in a parking lot filled with old weeds? A sign by the side of the parking lot said Half Moon Lane but there was no street. The bus inched past a rusty dumpster filled with garbage bags. Two men were unloading cartons at one of the warehouse loading docks, but they didn't even look up when the bus rolled past them.

The bus turned to face a brick wall at the back of the house. A faded mural on the wall featured an enormous box of *Black Mirror* chocolates, and underneath in peeling letters the words, *Satisfy Every Sweet Desire*. The wall had gaping cracks and was missing chunks of mortar. Faded pink insulation poked out from a stovepipe hole, beneath which there was a green door with a small brass doorknob.

The bus driver got up from his seat, stepped out of the bus and inserted an ornate key into one of the chocolates. Then he clambered back onto the bus. The bus jerked forward, its engine chortling. The box of chocolates began to melt away. Wil blinked his eyes. The bus was driving...right...through...the...wall.

Wil looked about wildly, but no one else seemed the least bit interested that they...they were driving right through a solid brick wall...into a long stone tunnel lit by lanterns. Wil turned to look back at Sophie. Her eyeglass frames were brilliant yellow. Hadn't they just been red and white polka dots? Wil looked down at Esme, shut his eyes for a moment and wished he could curl up tight inside her little hut.

Aunt Violet spoke from behind her handkerchief. "We're almost there and not a moment too soon, I'm sure."

The bus reached the end of the tunnel and Wil's eyes blinked in the bright sunlight as the bus rolled over two bumps. It turned into a narrow street lined with tall trees and large houses, many with peeling paint, lopsided porches and overgrown vines. At the end of the street, Wil saw a white house with a FOR SALE sign in front. The sign looked as if it were about to fall over.

The bus pulled up in front of a ramshackle brick house—built from a hodgepodge of twisted black, brown, pale yellow, burnt red and blue bricks. The stone path leading to the front door was overgrown with roses and raspberry brambles.

The bus driver rang the bell. "First stop—Half Moon Lane," he called. He tipped his hat to Aunt Violet. "I'll drop your luggage round later, if that's all right."

As Wil stepped down onto the sidewalk, Mr. Oystein waved his snake's head cane at Esme's cage. Then Wil heard him say to the driver, "Remember that boy I was telling you about, Mr. Scrimshaw—the one who had the snake on the train..."

"It's much cooler inside, Wil," said Aunt Rue. "I'll help Aunt Violet. She'll want to look at the garden. Sophie dear, could you get out some of the honey spice."

Wil edged his way through the raspberry brambles, up the steps to the porch and through the front door into a living room filled with worn stuffed chairs and a sofa. Beyond that was a bright kitchen in white and yellow. A grandfather clock in the corner chimed two, as Sophie clattered around in the kitchen.

Off the kitchen was a study lined in tall shelves overflowing with books. More books and papers were piled on the desk and the floor. Wil stood at the threshold of the study for a moment and breathed in the old, familiar musty smell of books.

"Well, here we are," said Aunt Rue, as she came through the back door into the kitchen. "Welcome to your new home, Wil."

"Thank you, Aunt Rue," said Wil, turning back to the kitchen.

But his aunt didn't seem to hear him. Instead of replying, she walked past him and shut the study door. Then she asked brightly, "Wil, perhaps you'd like some honey spice and fresh biscuits? I imagine you didn't sleep well on the train."

Suddenly overcome with dizziness, Wil swayed and almost dropped Esme's cage.

His aunt rested a cool hand on his forehead, and Wil smelled the sharp tang of ginger. She frowned. "Sophie, why don't you take Wil up to his room so he can rest. After all you've been through, poor boy—sleep as long as you want. We'll see you for dinner."

Barely able to put one foot in front of the other, Wil followed Sophie up the stairs with Esme's cage in his arms. His room was painted yellow and furnished with an empty bookshelf, a dresser and a cracked mirror. A wooden table and a chair stood beside the bed, which was covered in a blue checkered quilt. Wil set Esme's cage down on the table.

Sophie stood in the doorway, shifting awkwardly from one foot to the other.

"You know, I've never seen a snake like that," she said at last.

"Mr. Bertram gave Esme to me," said Will. "He has a bookstore near where I live, I mean where I used to live. She eats quail eggs."

"But her head's so small, how can she swallow an egg all at once?"

"Soph-eee," called Aunt Rue from the first floor.

"You can watch...but we have to get some eggs first," said Wil.

"Why does—" Sophie began to ask.

"Soph-eee..."

Sophie looked down the hallway then back at Esme. "I guess, I guess I'll see you at supper." Then she closed the door behind her.

Wil sat down on the bed and pulled the pouch from his pocket. Its metal links were as cool as Esme's skin. He hid the pouch under his mattress, and then lifted Esme from her cage. Her black eyes were shining and her tongue darted in the air. She coiled about his wrist to the tip of her tail.

"This is our new home, Esme," said Wil. Feeling bleak, he nestled under the covers with Esme curled up beside him.

Unbidden, the tears came, and Wil held Esme as if his life depended on it.

When the storm of sobs finally subsided, Wil stared out the bedroom window at the ghost moon in the blue sky and mused over all the things that had happened in the last week. The fire. His grandmother. Saying goodbye to Mr. Bertram. Esme loose on the train. Getting stuck in the washroom. The two green serpents guarding the door. The bus to MiddleGate, which had passed right through the brick house somehow—how could a bus do that, anyway?

Wil put Esme carefully back in her cage and sank into his pillow. His last thought before falling into a deep, deep sleep...who was the man at the train station? What news had he been waiting for, and why was time of the essence?

# VIII  A Question

*Have you ever seen a snake eat an egg?*

---

*SAEPE SECRETA OCCULTA NON MANENT DIU.*
**OFTEN, SECRETS DO NOT REMAIN SECRETS FOR LONG.**

---

Aunt Violet set her morning cup of tea down and plucked the wilted petals from the yellow roses on the kitchen table. "These roses aren't doing well in the heat," she said, as she propped up a drooping rose. "The poor boy must have been exhausted to sleep this long, Rue. What a scene when Esme set out to explore the train! How people do panic over things quite harmless. Someone fainted, and someone else—well, it was all rather diverting."

"No doubt it will take him a while to settle in," said Aunt Rue, stirring her tea.

"Rue, do you think he knows?" asked Aunt Violet.

Sophie looked up from playing with two hard-boiled eggs on the table. "Know what, Aunt Violet?"

Aunt Violet, who was still fussing over the drooping rose, did not answer Sophie.

"I'm sure he'll wake up when he's hungry," said Aunt Rue, ignoring both their questions.

Sophie picked up Cadmus from underneath the kitchen table and idly scratched his chin, while she eyed a bee buzzing around the pot of honey. "Do you know that Esme eats eggs?" Sophie asked. "I wonder how she can open her mouth wide enough to eat a whole egg." Then she asked again, "What does Wil not know?"

Cadmus chose that moment to jump from her lap onto the table. Lunging at the bee, he knocked Sophie's glass of milk to the floor.

"Cadmus, scat, you bad cat! Look what you've done now," squealed Sophie, and she tapped Cadmus on the nose.

Cadmus hissed and whirled from the room.

Aunt Rue stooped to pick up pieces of broken glass, and began mopping up the milk. "Snakes alive, my girl," she exclaimed, sounding thoroughly exasperated, "what do you think Wil doesn't know?"

# IX  Family Secrets

*There's no such thing as magic.*

---

*SEMEL DICTA VERBA NON REVENIUNT.*

WORDS, ONCE SAID, CANNOT BE TAKEN BACK.

---

Wil shielded his eyes against the glaring sun, pouring in through the bedroom window. His stomach was grumbling. I must have missed supper, he thought. He yawned and stretched.

Esme uncoiled herself from inside her hut.

"I'll get some eggs for you soon, Esme."

Esme gazed unblinking at Wil, even a bit reproachfully, he thought.

Feeling groggy, Wil padded out into the hallway and walked down the stairs. The kitchen door was open a crack. He heard Aunt Rue exclaim, "Snakes alive, girl, what do you think Wil doesn't know?"

What are they talking about? Wil wondered, and he pushed the door open.

Sophie, Aunt Rue and Aunt Violet looked up at him, obviously startled.

"Good morning, Wil," said Aunt Rue, who was the first to speak. Her voice was stiff. "You must be hungry after such a long sleep. Would you like some jam and toast, or a cup of warm milk?"

"Toast, please," said Wil. "And I think Esme is a little hungry too."

"Why don't you take Wil to the egg shop this afternoon, Sophie?" said Aunt Rue. "We need some more eggs for ourselves too." She bustled about, setting a place for Wil at the table. "School starts tomorrow, Wil, the first day of September. You've arrived at a perfect time. I've already spoken to the principal at Gruffud's Academy about your coming, and I've got two black school uniforms for you."

"Thank you, Aunt Rue." Wil toyed with his knife. "But...but...what is it I don't know?"

Nobody answered.

Wil turned to Sophie, but Sophie ducked her head and glanced over at Aunt Rue—who looked lost for words. Then Sophie looked at Aunt Violet. Aunt Violet was staring at the ceiling, however, seemingly transfixed by a long-legged spider in the corner above the stove. Sophie bit her lower lip and her eyeglass frames, which had been deep blue, turned slug-grey. Wil had the awful feeling that he came from a family of murderers.

"Our family, our family is, a—" Sophie paused.

"What?" asked Wil, convinced his worst fears were about to be confirmed.

"Um, we trace our family back ten generations," said Sophie, "and our family is one of the oldest."

"One of the oldest? The oldest what?" asked Wil, feeling puzzled.

"We can trace our ancestry way back to Britain. We're a mage family," Sophie blurted out all in one breath, as if someone were going to stop her from speaking.

"Mage?" Wil stared blankly at Sophie. "Mage family?" he repeated.

Sophie didn't reply. Instead, she looked over at Aunt Rue and then at Aunt Violet.

"Well, at least we're not murderers," said Wil, feeling vastly relieved.

Aunt Rue and Aunt Violet looked shocked.

Wil's mind raced back to when the bus had gone through the house with the five-pointed stars. The sick feeling in the pit of his stomach returned. Maybe he didn't come from a family of murderers, but coming from a family that was crazy seemed like the next-worst choice.

"Are you telling me that people here do magic?" He looked over at Aunt Rue and Aunt Violet, as if they would deny what Sophie had just told him.

"Well," said Aunt Violet and she leaned over to pat Wil's hand.

Wil pulled his hand away. "That's ridiculous! There's no such thing as magic."

Aunt Violet smiled weakly. "I don't suppose—"

"And why did Gran never tell me about you, anyway?" Wil interrupted, only dimly aware that his question was rather rude, since Aunt Rue and Aunt Violet were now his guardians.

"I'm sure your grandmother had her...her reasons, Wil," said Aunt Violet, who was cleaning her eyeglasses with her handkerchief—even though they were already clean, as far as Wil could tell.

Even as he asked why, he already knew the answer. *Magic—nothing but hocus-pocus bogus, William*, his grandmother would have snorted. *Don't believe a sorcerer's word of it, William.* No wonder his grandmother had never mentioned these relatives.

Before anyone else could speak, an eerie caterwauling echoed throughout the house. Sophie jumped up, knocking over one of the kitchen chairs, ran to the front door and yanked it open.

Wil followed Sophie.

"Cadmus," called Sophie, looking frantically around the front yard.

A thin, tense-looking woman who was wearing a straw hat was on her hands and knees weeding her garden next door. She ignored both Sophie and Wil.

"Cadmus...where are you?" said Sophie. She turned to the woman with the straw hat. "Mrs. Oleander, is Cadmus in your yard?"

"No," said Mrs. Oleander tersely, and she continued her weeding.

"Don't mind her," whispered Sophie, her eyeglass frames turning muddy-brown. "She hates Cadmus because he gets into fights with her tabby cat Calvino."

The caterwauling grew louder. "That sounds like it's coming from inside," said Sophie. Wil looked towards the house and saw a striped tail flicking at a windowpane...on the second floor...in a yellow room.

"Sophie, Esme—" Wil's voice choked.

"If your snake hurts my cat—" said Sophie.

# X The Serpent's Chain

*Beware.*

---

*IN UMBRA MAGNAE CATENAE STANT.*

**THEY STAND IN THE SHADOW OF A GREAT CHAIN.**

---

Wil ran to his bedroom, followed by Sophie. Frozen, they stared at the scene before them.

Unblinking...whiskers quivering...Cadmus was about to pounce. The tip of his tail...twitched...once...twice.

Body coiling, scales rasping across the floor, Esme's head arched—her lidless eyes fixed on the cat's black face. Her mouth gaped pink and she hissed. Never had Esme looked so formidable, thought Wil.

Esme lunged at Cadmus—

"Cadmus, no!" shrieked Sophie and she grabbed Cadmus's tail.

Cadmus hissed, slipped from Sophie's grasp and raced out the door.

In a wink, Esme slithered up Wil's bedstead.

"Sophie, help me lift up the mattress, so Wil can get Esme," said Aunt Rue.

As Wil pulled Esme out, his hand brushed against the hidden pouch, which fell to the floor. Out rolled the black medallion; it spun in a circle and stopped before a breathless Aunt Violet, who had just entered the room.

Everyone stared at the medallion with its tiny, glowing serpent.

Aunt Violet bent down and touched the medallion, but pulled her hand away. Slumping, she moaned, "Burning..."

"Aunt Violet!" shrieked Aunt Rue.

But Aunt Violet's eyes were closed. Her skin turned pasty white.

"Sophie, quick!" said Aunt Rue. "Peppermint oil in the cupboard."

Aunt Violet's voice began to quaver.

> *Who breaks the Serpent's Chain*
> *Recoil not from earthly pain.*
> *Who seeks to save the multitude*
> *Only friendship and gratitude*
> *Shall break the Serpent's Chain.*

Then she whispered in a deep, hoarse voice—not Aunt Violet's voice at all—*Beware the Serpent's Chain.*

———⚬———

Sophie clutched the bottle of peppermint oil. Her spine tingled. She looked at Wil, but he was rigid, as if in shock, Esme coiled around his wrist.

"Sophie, the peppermint," exclaimed Aunt Rue. "Don't just stand there, my girl."

"Sorry, Aunt Rue."

Sophie held the peppermint under Aunt Violet's nose. Aunt Violet coughed, her eyelids fluttered and with Aunt Rue's help, she sat up and looked curiously at the medallion.

"Where did this come from?" Aunt Violet asked.

Wil picked up the medallion. "I—" He took a breath. "I don't know. Gran gave it to me," said Wil and he drew the gold ring from the pouch, "along with this ring."

"Aunt Violet, why did you say, *Beware the Serpent's Chain*? What's the Serpent's Chain?" asked Sophie.

But Aunt Rue and Aunt Violet seemed to be staring right through Wil and did not answer.

# XI Egg Museum

*Do not touch the eggs.*

---

*ANIMAL EX OVO NASCITUR. CAVE OVUM CAERULEUM.*
LIVING THINGS COME FROM EGGS, BUT BEWARE BLUE EGGS.

---

"The egg shop isn't far," said Sophie as she and Wil left the house. "Just past Grunion Square."

Wil nodded and looked down Half Moon Lane to the right, towards the large, white house at the end of the street. Its FOR SALE sign seemed to be leaning over more than ever.

"Have you ever been inside the house that's for sale?" asked Wil.

"I tried once, but the door was locked and the house is so creepy—no one's lived in it for years," said Sophie.

They walked past Earbend Street, Wog's Hollow and Rolling Fork Street...all of them lined with tilting houses.

"Why are all the houses so crooked in MiddleGate? I mean, they're really—" Wil said, then stopped, afraid that Sophie would feel insulted.

Sophie only laughed. "You should see the houses on the other side of the river. They're even more crooked. It's the mud—the houses are sinking." She whisked a piece of white chalk from her pocket and stopped to draw a large spiral snake on the sidewalk.

Wil stood watching her and blurted out. "I still don't understand how we got here. You know, how did we...we had to...we went right through that brick wall, and the box of chocolates melted."

"You mean the gate to enter MiddleGate?" asked Sophie, her tone of voice slightly defensive.

"Yes," said Wil. "It's impossible! You can't just go through a brick wall like that."

"But we did, so it's not impossible, is it?" said Sophie, her voice steely, as she drew a forked tongue on the snake.

Wil decided to leave the brick wall alone.

Three more blocks, and Half Moon Lane ended at Stricker Street. Despite the cloying heat, Stricker Street was crowded with people. Small shops, benches and hanging flowerpots lined the sidewalk, and the smell of cinnamon buns and fresh bread filled the air, making Wil's mouth water. They passed a large storefront window filled with gleaming jars of honey. Then the smell of roses, lemon and peppermint drifting out from a soap shop caused Wil to sneeze no less than nine times. By the time he'd stopped sneezing, they were already turning onto another street. Far in the distance loomed a monument in the middle of an enormous stone plaza. That must be Grunion Square, thought Wil. As they drew closer, he saw two bronze snakes rising up out of large boulders and coiling around each other. Small children were climbing the snakes and waving at their parents below.

Wil was so impressed by the size of the snakes—the children riding their backs seemed to be flying—he suddenly realized he hadn't heard a word Sophie said.

"...and thousands of them have been murdered," said Sophie.

"Murdered?" said Wil, trying to pick up the conversation.

"Yes, the snakes of Narcisse. They winter over in the caves, thousands and thousands of them. We're going to see them the end of this month. Have you been listening?" Sophie asked, her voice impatient.

"I was looking at the snakes."

"The Brimstone Snakes? I used to ride them when I was young too," said Sophie, hardly looking at the monument. "Maybe Aunt Rue will find out what's going on. She works in the Department of Endangered Insects in the Secretariat, and they've called an emergency meeting today."

Wil began to feel quite stupid and stopped to do up one of his shoelaces. "Secretariat—what's that?"

"The Secretariat on the Status of Magical Creatures—they're responsible for the safekeeping of all magical creatures." Sophie stepped carefully over a long crack in the sidewalk. "Some people believe the Narcisse snakes are immortal."

"How can snakes be immortal? That doesn't make sense."

"I don't know," said Sophie. "I looked up the Serpent's Chain in one of my father's old books this morning before everybody was awake, but didn't find much. I'm not allowed in his study, anyway. Aunt Rue thinks I'll mess it up."

"When did your father disappear?" asked Wil.

"It's been ten years—practically since I was born." Sophie scuffed a pebble from the sidewalk. "The Official Register says he's deceased."

"Didn't they search the study for clues after he disappeared?"

"I guess they didn't find anything. Aunt Violet never gives up hope, and Aunt Rue lights a candle for him every night." Sophie was silent for a moment, and then out of the blue said, "And Aunt Rue never even mentions your mother Ivy. Do you know why?"

"Just because they were sisters—" said Wil, wondering what Sophie was hinting at. "I mean, maybe they didn't get along."

"It's not just that," said Sophie in a dark tone. "Aunt Rue says their mother was heartbroken when Ivy left. Their mother died soon after. So it was all your mother's fault."

"What do you mean it was her fault?" said Wil, hardly knowing what to make of all this.

"She married an outsider," said Sophie, and she stepped right on a crack in the sidewalk.

"An outsider?" asked Wil, beginning to feel annoyed that Sophie seemed to be blaming him for something that his parents had done— something that happened long before he was even born. "What's being an outsider got to do with anything?"

"Your father was from a non-magical family," said Sophie.

Sophie's matter-of-fact tone was unnerving. "That's ridiculous," said Wil. "Just because you're magical or non-magical doesn't mean you can't...you can't marry someone, does it? And I don't even remember my mother and father. They died when I was really young, and Gran didn't tell me much about them." He felt a lump in his throat at the thought of Gran and swallowed hard. "Your dad—ten years is a long time, isn't it? And what...what happened to your mother?"

**35**

"Ten years doesn't mean he's dead, you know," Sophie said. Her voice cracked, and the frames of her glasses changed swiftly from marbled blue to an angry orange. "My father was one of the teachers at Gruffud's; he taught verbology. And my mother left when I was a baby."

"She left?" repeated Wil. "Why would your mother leave you?"

"Aunt Rue says she turned strange after my father disappeared. Everyone was talking. They accused her of covering up for him. She couldn't take it anymore, I guess," said Sophie. "Anyway, I did manage to look through three books in my father's study, and they didn't even mention the Serpent's Chain. Only *The Wizard's Companion* listed it."

"So what did it say?" asked Wil, still pondering why Aunt Rue never mentioned his mother. He kicked a stone down the sidewalk. It ricocheted off the side of a building down into a grate and there was the sound of a splash far below.

"The Serpent's Chain used to be called Catena Serpentis. It was a secret society."

"A secret society?"

"*The Wizard's Companion* didn't say much—only that they probably used snakes in some of their ceremonies. But that's hundreds of years ago, and the society was abolished. Why would Aunt Violet talk about something that hasn't been around for centuries? And what would it have to do with your black medallion?"

"Wasn't it weird how she fainted after touching the medallion?" said Will. "And then that really creepy voice...*Beware the Serpent's Chain.*"

"Yeah, it was weird," said Sophie. "Come on, we've got to go here, along Groaning Creek Road." She turned right off onto a small side street and pointed to a large brick building in the distance. "Gruffud's is over there—see that building with the four towers and the clock? We'll finally get to do some real magic. At my junior school, they wouldn't let us do anything."

"You have to wait to do magic until you go to Gruffud's?" asked Wil, surprised.

"Even then, we're only allowed to practise on Gruffud's grounds. After we pass the qualifying exams in grade eleven, we can practise anywhere in MiddleGate—actually, anywhere in the country. But if you're caught off school grounds, without permission—"

"What happens?" asked Wil. "How would anyone know?"

Sophie frowned. "I don't know," she said slowly, "but I've heard the Firecatchers question you." She shuddered.

"What are Firecatchers?' asked Wil.

"They wear long red cloaks, and you can't see their faces. They're like our guardians," said Sophie, again as if she were stating the obvious.

"Guardians—what do they guard?" asked Wil.

Sophie laughed. "You make it sound like they're guarding treasure or something. They enforce the laws."

Wil was about to ask more questions about the Firecatchers, but Sophie stopped suddenly in front of a squat, whitewashed building. Hanging outside was a large oval sign:

AUGUSTUS LEOPOLD EGBERTINE & SON
Musée des Oeufs
*Exceptional, Exemplary and Exotic Eggs*

On the door of the shop dangled a stern notice in red letters:

*DO NOT TOUCH THE EGGS*
*Défense de toucher aux oeufs*

Sophie turned the brass doorknob. A whoosh of cool air greeted them as they entered the shop.

"That's Mr. Egbertine behind the counter...and his son Auguste standing beside him," whispered Sophie.

Mr. Egbertine was remarkably like an egg himself; the top of his pate was shiny and mottled. He was polishing a clutch of green speckled eggs while talking with Mr. Oystein, the man with the snake's head cane. Just as Sophie and Wil approached the counter, Auguste—who sported a head of carrot-orange hair, which had begun to recede—slipped into the back of the shop behind a curtain of swaying, white oval beads.

"Do you have any quail eggs, Mr. Egbertine?" asked Sophie. "This is my cousin Wil, and he has a snake that eats quail eggs."

"*Un moment, mes petits*," said Mr. Egbertine, smiling at the children. He turned back to Mr. Oystein. "Perhaps the reports about the extermination are exaggerated, *non*?"

"Inconceivable that the caves have been desecrated," said Mr. Oystein. He thumped his cane on the floor. "But who could have done it?"

"There should have been an exhaustive inquiry a year ago," murmured Mr. Egbertine. He rubbed his own head absent-mindedly with the polishing cloth and his voice grew more strident. "At any rate, about that licence, it's well past the season, *je pense*." Mr. Egbertine donned a pair of wire eyeglasses, and squinted up at an egg chart hanging on the wall behind the counter. "I'm afraid the season ended two months ago," he said firmly. "No one is exempt, *personne*."

"These confounded regulations!" exclaimed Mr. Oystein. "Why, when we were boys, remember—"

"That's no justification for how things are now, Oskar Oystein, *n'est-ce pas*?" interrupted Mr. Egbertine, and he waggled his polishing cloth near Mr. Oystein's face. "If things had been regulated then, we wouldn't be where we are today, would we? Inexcusable greed, that's what it is."

At the word *greed*, Mr. Egbertine placed one of the freshly polished eggs back in the basket, but not gently enough. Green yolk splattered Mr. Oystein's face and oozed over the counter. Wil's nose wrinkled at the pungent smell.

Sophie leaned over to Wil and whispered, "Let's go find Esme's eggs ourselves."

They wandered over to look at the eggs in the glass cases. The largest one was deep blue in colour—very rare, according to the sign.

"*Firebird Egg Donated by Vitellus Albumen*," read Wil.

The shop door slammed open suddenly—so loudly that Auguste came running out from the back of the shop.

A woman wearing a flowered pink and orange frilly apron marched to the counter and thrust a basket filled with broken eggshells under Mr. Egbertine's very nose.

Mr. Egbertine, looking alarmed as he eyed the broken eggshells, broke off his conversation with Mr. Oystein. "Mrs. Blancheflour, welcome. How are we today? Is there some problem?" he asked.

Mrs. Blancheflour's eyes flashed. "Mr. Egbertine, a problem!" She paused to catch her breath. "Do you know who is coming to my afternoon tea? And I have no eggs."

Mr. Egbertine patted her arm. "Dear Mrs. Blancheflour, do please calm yourself. Would you like to sit down?"

Mrs. Blancheflour ignored Auguste's offer of a chair. Her voice only continued to rise. "You have no idea what a trouble this has been!"

Wil leaned forward to hear what else Mrs. Blancheflour was going to say. As he did so, he felt the glass beneath him creak dangerously. He tried to pull himself up, but it was too late. The glass case holding the large eggs cracked, and Wil fell to the floor amidst broken glass and eggshells. The pungent smell of skunk, rotting swamp and burnt toast filled his nostrils. Leaving the irate Mrs. Blancheflour to Auguste and Mr. Oystein, Mr. Egbertine hurried over. "Oh, *mon bleu!* Such a mess! *Mes oeufs...qu'est-ce que tu as fait?*"

Still scolding, Mr. Egbertine tried to help Wil to his feet but lost his balance, knocked into Sophie and tumbled right on top of Wil.

Mr. Egbertine's head smashed the last, unbroken egg—the deep-blue firebird egg. Blue yolk oozed slowly from the cracked shell and began to bubble and sizzle. Blue vapour swirled through the air and filled the shop. Wil could scarcely breathe under Mr. Egbertine's weight. He felt as if everything were moving in slow motion.

Mr. Oystein, Mrs. Blancheflour and Auguste tried to help Wil, Sophie and Mr. Egbertine up, but the blue vapour soon overcame them too. Finally, Mrs. Blancheflour managed to stagger to her feet and made a crooked exit, obviously having forgotten that she needed more eggs at all. Mr. Oystein left too, mumbling incoherently about fires and birds, and Auguste dabbed a cloth at the blue ooze on his father's forehead. But his father only pushed him away.

"Not now, Augushhhte."

Wil and Sophie managed to stand up together, each leaning against the other, with blue yolk dribbling down their faces.

Mr. Egbertine waved his hands to clear the air. "Shho lucky that firebird egg didn't exshhhplode, by sherpent's grace. Now, Sh-sh-ophie, shhhquail eggshh you need? Exshceptional, these eggs. Let me know how the little shnake likeshh them. And here'sh a shpecial bashket for your aunt."

# XII Breakfast for Three

*The egg looked far too big.*

---

*NUMQUAM NIMIS OVA.*

YOU CAN NEVER HAVE TOO MANY EGGS.

---

W il awoke in a cold sweat. Grey drops of rain were beading against the window, and it took him a moment to remember where he was. He had been dreaming that he was unpacking a box at Pirsstle and Bertram's. He peeled away layer after layer of brown paper wrapping, but every time he pulled one layer of paper off...there was another one underneath.

A knock at the bedroom door and Aunt Rue's muffled "Time to get up, Wil" reminded him it was the first day of school.

"All right," he called, and he felt a knot of worry form in his stomach. He dressed quickly, then reached under his bed and pulled out the metal pouch. The black medallion and gold ring were still safely inside.

"Sophie...Wil...breakfast. Hurry up, both of you," called Aunt Rue.

"Coming, Aunt Rue," answered Wil. He pulled on his socks. "So what if I don't believe in magic? There's got to be a logical explanation for everything," he muttered. "That house with the stars must be some sort of camouflage."

He slipped the medallion and ring onto the chain, and quickly fastened it around his neck.

He tied up his shoelaces. "You'd better watch it—talking to yourself—or people will think you're crazy!"

Aunt Rue and Aunt Violet cajoled Sophie and Wil to eat a steaming bowl of porridge, but Sophie only picked away at the porridge and complained that she wasn't hungry. Wil, who was still feeling woozy, ate only a mouthful or two, as he gazed out the kitchen window at an ugly stone gargoyle in the back garden. It had a long spiral tail and was hunched over as if it were hiding something.

Wil suddenly remembered Esme had not had her egg yet, for Aunt Rue had taken one look at them when they returned from the Egg Museum and popped them straight into bed with warm soup.

"Sophie, do you want to watch Esme eat her egg?" asked Wil.

Sophie nodded.

"Don't dawdle," said Aunt Rue, "or you'll both be late for school, and it's starting to spit rain."

———

Esme had burrowed into the earth in her cage. Just her head was poking out. When Wil put one of the quail eggs in her cage, her eyes fixed on it.

"I don't see how she can put that whole thing in her mouth," said Sophie. Even though she knew snakes' jaws were hinged, the egg looked far too big for Esme's delicate little mouth.

Esme slithered out and circled the egg.

"What's she doing?" asked Sophie.

"Sshhh, watch," said Wil.

Esme lunged at the egg, her mouth wide open. She nudged the egg, and her mouth snapped around it. Her scales stretched so tautly around the egg that Sophie thought she looked like a long polliwog with an oversized head.

There was a small cracking sound.

"What's that?" asked Sophie.

"That's the egg inside," said Wil.

Esme waved from side to side.

"She's crushing it," said Wil.

Esme gaped and regurgitated a flat pellet of crushed eggshell.

"Yuck, that's gross," said Sophie, leaning closer to take a better look. Perhaps having Wil and Esme around would be all right after all, she thought.

41

# XIII First Day

*Tibi admitto.*

---

*NUMQUAM IN STERCUS INGREDERE.*
NEVER STEP IN DUNG!

---

By the time Wil and Sophie left the house, they had to hurry. The snakes in Grunion Square were glistening in what was now a steady drizzle. As they walked quickly, Sophie regaled Wil with what she'd heard about some of the teachers.

"The one you'll have to watch out for is Mage Adderson. Everyone says she's got a real temper."

As they drew closer and closer to Gruffud's, the knot in Wil's stomach grew. He would have liked to see his old teacher Mrs. Eardley again, even if she was obsessed with brain music. He could hear her flat voice in his head. "Researchers have recently discovered that music increases a student's powers of concentration." Whenever Mrs. Eardley played music in class, though, Wil had forgotten to do whatever it was he was supposed to do, and listened to the music instead. Maybe it depended on the kind of—

"Wil, watch out—" Sophie said.

With a sinking heart, Wil felt something squishy under his shoe. The unmistakable smell of dog droppings wafted to his nose.

Sophie found a stick for Wil to scrape his shoes clean and then stood off at a distance by a lamppost, holding her nose.

"We're going to be really late," she said, "and it's only our first day."

Even as Sophie spoke, a bell sounded nine gongs.

The wet streets were completely deserted by the time they neared the school, but Wil's feet slowed as they passed by a building with colossal columns and an arched entrance.

MIDDLEGATE LIBRARY ~
THE FISHER RARE BOOK COLLECTION

On either side of the library's doors were two stone serpents—one had a lion's head, the other, an eagle's head.

"Wil, come on, you can see the library later," said Sophie impatiently. "We're really late."

Wil followed Sophie past a great boulder and up the steps of a towering stone building with mullioned windows covered in vines. Beneath a column just inside the entrance stood a woman dressed in long grey robes. Above her, two stone faces with long braids stared from the top of the column. Looking more closely, Wil noticed that the braids were snakes and one of the faces had a beard of snakes.

"Miss Isidor, I believe. Perhaps you weren't aware that matins begin at nine bells?" said the woman, staring grimly at Sophie.

Sophie seemed to shrink, and didn't say anything.

"It was my fault," Wil said, "I mean—" He glanced over at Sophie whose bottom lip was trembling. "I'm sorry; we didn't mean—" Wil's voice faltered under the woman's unrelenting stare. Unconsciously, he reached for the black medallion and gold ring around his neck.

The woman's nose wrinkled. Her sharp eyes glanced down at Wil's shoes.

"This is my cousin, William Wychwood," Sophie mustered in a small voice.

"Ah, yes. Welcome to Gruffud's Academy, Mr. Wychwood," said the woman. "In future, I trust you'll be on time." Her eyes flickered over Wil's medallion and ring. "Also, we do not encourage the wearing of any jewellery during school hours." With these words, she turned and strode down the corridor.

"Who's that?" asked Wil.

"Mage Adderson—the teacher I told you about. She teaches numeristics," said Sophie. She glanced above Wil's head, and put her finger to her lips. "Sshhh."

Wil looked up. One of the stone faces was staring right at him, and if he was not mistaken, one of its snake braids was actually twitching.

———

The ceilings of Stone Hall reverberated with the chatter of several hundred students, who were all wearing black uniforms and colourful sashes. Wil gazed up in awe at Stone Hall, which was lined in tall columns. Carved stone gargoyles with hairy pointed ears and gnashing teeth leered at the students from every direction, as if to say, *We're watching you.*

"Grade fives are seated in the first three front rows," said a man who was no taller than Wil and had a bushy white beard divided into three braids. The man pointed to the front of the hall, and Wil caught a glimpse of a brown serpent tattoo coiling from the man's left wrist to his middle finger.

"Each grade has its own colours," whispered Sophie, as she and Wil squeezed into their places on the benches. "Grade fives wear red sashes with a white stripe, grade sixes wear orange and white, sevens wear yellow and white and I think the eights are green and white."

"What about the black and white sashes?" Wil asked, but Sophie was already talking with two girls.

A tall, broad-shouldered woman wearing a purple robe stepped to the front of the hall. Mage Adderson stood behind her with what must have been the other teachers.

Stone Hall went silent.

The woman gazed out over all the students.

"I am Mage Agassiz, the principal of Gruffud's Academy. Today we welcome all our students, new and old, to yet another year at Gruffud's. I trust each of you enjoyed your summers and are ready to take up your training."

A tall girl with curly hair standing next to Wil jostled his elbow. "Something really stinks." She wrinkled her nose and inched away from Wil.

Wil tried to draw his feet in under him, but those sitting around him began to murmur about a disgusting smell.

"...each year since the beginning, we commence the first matins of term with Gruffud's Chant," continued Mage Agassiz. "When the Chant ends, all be seated but for the grade fives. Grade fives will step forward, one by one, to receive their sashes. All of you shall then proceed to your individual classrooms upon ceremony's end to meet your teachers and embark on your studies. We break at twelve noon for lunch, and after that reconvene for afternoon classes at one o'clock.

"Students are reminded that they shall not practise the magical arts beyond the bounds of Gruffud's. The clock tower is off-limits. Students are also reminded that the school lands along the riverbank are strictly forbidden, as the waters can be treacherous.

"Finally, Mr. and Mrs. Pyper, our school caretakers—" Mage Agassiz gestured towards a plump woman with white hair and a broad smile on her flushed pink face, and a thin stooped man who looked much older, both of them standing by the side door. "Our school caretakers want me to remind you that they would appreciate your keeping your desks and lockers clean. There will be no practising of magic in the hallways—the classrooms and study rooms are to be used for this purpose—and eating is allowed only in the west wing of Stone Hall.

"I know you will uphold the honour of Gruffud's Academy during this, our four hundred and ninety-fourth year. Please stand."

Hundreds of feet shuffled as everyone stood up.

Mage Agassiz raised her hand for a moment, and then brought it down.

Voices soared into the air and a swell of sound filled Stone Hall.

> *Um-bris nos de-da-mus.*
> *Um-bris nos de-da-mus.*

Wil didn't understand what the song meant. It sounded like Latin, which he had never liked—there was too much to memorize—but he shivered as he listened to the voices echoing each other back and forth, round after round.

When the last note of the chant finally died away, a long silence filled Stone Hall.

Mage Adderson then stepped forward, cleared her throat and held up a list. "When your name is called, please step forward to receive your sash."

"Maia Amorante.

"And Meena Amorante."

Twin sisters—both had long black hair falling below their waists and it was impossible to tell which one was which.

"Jinzhen Cheng."

Jinzhen Cheng was a small boy with jet-black straight hair. He walked with quick steps to the front.

"Olin Cramer."

Olin Cramer strutted to the front as if he, and not Mage Adderson, were giving out the sashes himself.

Mage Adderson continued to read name after name.

"Sophie Isidor."

Sophie practically danced to the front to receive her sash. She was beaming when she turned around.

"Merrily Klimchak."

Merrily Klimchak's long brown hair covered her face so that Wil couldn't see her expression.

"Regina Piehard."

A small, thin girl with a sour, pinched expression on her face sidled to the front. She turned and waved to the tall, curly-haired girl standing right beside Wil.

"Sygnithia Sly."

Pinching her nose, the girl beside Wil said in a loud nasally whisper, "Ex-c-u-u-u-se me," as she passed Wil.

"Sylvain Sly."

Sylvain Sly must have been Sygnithia's twin brother. They both had the same large build, round blue eyes and curly black hair, and Sylvain was at least a head taller than Wil.

"Harley Weeks."

Harley Weeks's round face looked like it had a permanent smile pasted onto it.

I'm next, thought Wil, wishing he could sink through the stone floor.

"William Wychwood."

It seemed to take Wil forever to shuffle to the front. Mage Agassiz held the red and white sash above his head.

What if she smells my shoes? Wil saw Mage Agassiz's nostrils flare...and held his breath. What if she doesn't give me a sash?

Then the sash came down over his head, the satin cooling his cheek.

"William Wychwood, *tibi admitto ad collegiam.*"

# XIV  Lips of the Stung

*The letters all whisked about.*

---

*SI LINGUA ERRAT, CARMEN PERIT.*
SLIP OF THE TONGUE, THE CHARM'S UNDONE.

---

The first morning's class—numeristics with Mage Adderson—
was held at the end of a long, dim hallway lined in wood panelling.

Mage Adderson was already writing a series of numbers on
the board.

2 3 5 7 11 13 17 19 23
29 31 37 41 43 47 53 59 61
67 71 73 79 83 89 97 101

She turned to face the class.

"Numeristics has an ancient history. No one should leave Gruffud's
without a deep appreciation of the numeric arts and the significance of
numbers in human affairs. We could, for instance, take no pleasure in
music without numeristics, for music is but a form of unconscious arith-
metic. Now, can anyone tell me why these numbers are special?"

When it was clear that no one in the class was going to answer, Mage Adderson said slowly, "These are all prime numbers. Does anyone know what a prime number is?"

Silence.

Mage Adderson's dark eyes gleamed. "Perhaps you should be taking notes?"

There was a flurry of papers, and pencils appeared from pockets. Everyone began to scratch busily in notebooks.

"Yes, a prime number—since none of you seem to know, hard as that is to believe—a prime number is a natural number, such as 1, 2, 3 and so on—but greater than 1—that can be divided evenly only by 1 and itself. Prime numbers are particularly powerful."

———

The verbology teacher was Mage Terpsy, a plump woman with watery eyes—one brilliant blue and one muddy brown—magnified by triangular eyeglasses.

"Everyone, please take out your workbooks," said Mage Terpsy, "and write down the letters of the alphabet in order."

"Aren't we supposed to know the alphabet by now?" Wil whispered to Sophie.

Sophie only shrugged and shook her head, looking as puzzled as he did.

Mage Terpsy pointed to a piece of chalk, which rose into the air and began to print the alphabet on the board all by itself.

Impossible, Wil thought.

"Let's juggle these letters about, shall we?" Mage Terpsy waved her hand once in a circle.

"*Mixusfixus.*"

The letters on the board began to jerk. The *L* jostled next to the *K*, and the *Y* jumped to the end of the line. The *Z* and the *I* sallied up to each other and switched places abruptly.

Wil blinked his eyes. There, on the board was a sentence.

*The five boxing wizards jump quickly.*

"Thirty-one letters in all," said Mage Terpsy. "We've used every letter of the alphabet; and the ninth letter of the alphabet has been used four times."

Mage Terpsy drew another circle in the air. "*Mixusfixus.*"
This time, the letters whisked about even more quickly and another sentence appeared.

> *Sphinx of black quartz, judge my vow.*

"Twenty-nine letters, that one. Of course you may want to go for a more common sort of sentence." "*Mixusfixus!*"
The letters swirled about in a frenzied circle on the board.

> *The quick brown fox jumps over the lazy dog.*

"Thirty-five letters with some repetition, particularly with the three *E*s and four *O*s. *Mixusfixus*—the simplest of word charms, but it can be quite effective for unscrambling letters, among other more complex uses," Mage Terpsy said brightly, blinking as she looked around at the class. "Pangrams such as these use every letter of the alphabet.

"Now take your alphabets, please. Concentrate, draw a circle in the air—make sure it's counter-clockwise—and say firmly, '*Mixusfixus*.' I won't expect you to use all the letters at this stage, but I think you will come up with some originals in time."

After watching everyone else waving their hands about, Wil took a breath and drew a circle in the air. "*Mixus-fixt-us*," he said, stumbling over the last letters.

Nothing happened.

He tried again, "*Mixusfixus.*" To his surprise, the letter *B* jerked and jumped, like a sardine flopping over.

He looked over at Sophie with a grin and saw she had already managed to coax the beginnings of a small sentence from her letters.

"I think you're messing a litter in your alphabet, my dear," said Mage Terpsy.

Wil looked at Mage Terpsy's blue eye as she bent over his workbook. She must have meant *missing a letter*.

"Yes, where's your *W*?" asked Mage Terpsy. "At this stage, it really won't work unless you have all the letters there." Mage Terpsy clapped her hands. "Everyone, hiss and lear! Make sure your alphabet is complete. Slubberdegullions, all of you, if you do not have command of your letters. An important part of spells, need I say it, is...s-p-e-l-l-i-n-g." She laughed at her own pun, then her eyes sharpened. "I dare say you will be hard put to practise your charms and incantations without complete control of your tongue. A half-formed wish is the same as a half-warmed fish—and beware lips of the stung."

"'Lips of the stung,'" Wil murmured to himself. What was she talking about?

"We will be learning many ways to flex your imaginations, and—"

A sharp crackle at the back of the class interrupted Mage Terpsy. Olin Cramer was desperately trying to blow out a fire in his workbook. Mage Terpsy hurried over and somehow—out of thin air—conjured a beaker of water, which she splashed on the workbook. There was a sizzling sound and the foul smell of smoke.

"You must have drawn your circle in the air clockwise, rather than counter-clockwise—Mr. Cramer, is it? A good lesson for everyone—the letters merely became confused and began to burn.

"Now, for homework, please prepare five sentences that use up as many letters of the alphabet as possible. Also, for next class, please read the first ten pages of *Magykal Spelling, Grammar and Palaver* by Blaesius Balbulus."

# XV  The Gatekeeper

*What are you staring at?*

---

*RES QUAE PER SE ABEUNT PER SE REDIBUNT.*

THINGS THAT DISAPPEAR BY THEMSELVES
CAN COME BACK BY THEMSELVES.

---

The afternoon began with Mage Adderson escorting them down steep steps at the back of Stone Hall to a tunnel leading to the library. Lanterns cast long shadows on the damp, stone walls. The stone floor was uneven, and Wil pitched forward into Sylvain, who turned around and gave him a nasty look.

The library had high vaulted ceilings, thick carpets, dark polished tables, broad benches and stained glass windows. The globular lamps on the rectangular tables and the chandelier hanging down like some brooding spider did little to lift the sense of dim. But the gleaming wooden shelves took Wil's breath away. Row upon row of books—more than he could read in a whole lifetime.

Mage Adderson picked up a tiny silver bell sitting on the counter. It tinkled merrily.

A plump woman, dressed completely in white, emerged from a back room.

"Class, this is Miss Heese," Mage Adderson said tersely. Muttering something about a meeting to attend, she hurried off.

Miss Heese's head seemed overly large for her body—an effect magnified by her white, curly hair, which reminded Wil of dandelion fluff—and she wore rectangular, white-framed eyeglasses. She spoke in such a hoarse, raspy voice that Wil had to strain to hear her.

"Welcome to MiddleGate Library, grade fivesss," said Miss Heese, with a peculiar hissing sound that reminded Wil of water sizzling on a hot, oiled fry pan. "The MiddleGate Library is one of the country's finessst, and scholars from all over the world visit usss..."

Wil's eyes strayed to the line of pale marble busts on top of the library shelves. Their eyes were blank and sightless. Then he noticed a fat leather-bound book lying on top of the shelving cart right beside him— *The Golden Wing: A History of All Creatures Magykal*. He started to leaf through the book to see if it had anything about the Serpent's Chain—

"What seek you?" said a small whisper in his right ear.

Wil looked around quickly in the direction of the voice. But there was no one standing beside him. He quickly replaced the volume back on the cart.

"The boy standing by the shelving cart—" said Miss Heese, pointing her finger at Wil. "You were just looking at *The Golden Wing: A History of All Creatures Magykal*. What is your name?"

"Wil Wychwood," whispered Wil, and several of the other students tittered.

Miss Heese smiled for the first time. "Ah, William Wychwood, I'm sure we'll become good friends, you and I. You like booksss, don't you?"

Wil nodded numbly, and several other students sniggered.

"Now children, the library bell rings ten minutesss prior to closing time."

As Miss Heese said this, a tower of books sitting on the counter lifted itself into the air.

Everyone's gaze swivelled to the tower of books. If Miss Heese noticed that some of the students were pointing at the books suspended above the counter, she gave no indication.

"We have four simple rulesss in this library."

The tower of books floated slowly back down to the counter. Then the small silver bell sitting on the counter rose into the air, but Miss Heese did not seem to notice—either that, or she was completely ignoring it. She continued in her raspy whisper.

"Rule No. 1: No noissse. The library is a place for quiet study and contemplation. It is not a place for loud conversation, coughing or sneezing."

At this, the bell began to tinkle.

Miss Heese whipped about, grabbed the bell and slammed it down on the counter. She patted her hair down, drew out a pink handkerchief from the sleeve of her robe and dabbed at her nose. With a sniff, she held out her hand and pointed mid-air. "May I introduce you to the library's official ghossst, by the name of Peerslie."

Everyone turned to Peerslie, or at least in the direction of where the bell had been hanging. Wil couldn't see any ghost, but then perhaps you weren't supposed to see it. From the looks on everyone's faces, no one else could see Peerslie either.

"Everyone calls him Peeping Peerslie," Sophie whispered to Wil.

The ghost must have been angry because it refused to make its presence known any further.

Miss Heese sniffed once more, and returned to the rules.

"Rule No. 2: no writing in any of the books. Rule No. 3: no tearing or cutting pages from the books. Rule No. 4: do not reshelve the books. These four rules ensure that the integrity of our collection is not compromised. We hope these instructions are clear. Now, let's see where the reserved books are for your classes."

Sophie whispered to Wil, "Why does she always say *we* when there's only *one* of her?"

"Who cares?" said Wil. "Do you realize how many books there are here? And is there really a ghost? Why is he called Peeping Peerslie and why can't I see him?"

"He's invisible, but he's always peeping over people's shoulders and trying to do their homework," Sophie answered. "Aunt Violet told me he's been here practically since the beginning."

---

In cartology, high wooden stools perched behind long tables. Maps papered the entire room, and the ceiling was covered with star charts.

Standing at the front of the class was Mage Tibor. He was wearing half-spectacles, tinted a deep blue, which threatened to slip off his nose at any moment.

"Cartology is an exact science that requires sublime knowledge of the Earth's contours...hmmm, extremities of the Earth's crust...hmmm, knowledge of secret doors and gates."

Wil opened his notebook and began to jot down notes about secret doors and gates—he wondered whether he could ask Mage Tibor about the house with the five-pointed stars—but as Mage Tibor's voice droned on and on about "precise attention to detail," Wil had to pinch himself to keep awake.

———

Botanicals with Mage Radix followed in the Gruffud's greenhouse, which looked like a miniature domed glass palace. Mage Radix, a broad-shouldered man, stout as he was tall, stepped nimbly down the long rows of plants. The greenhouse was so hot and humid that Wil began to feel faint during Mage Radix's lecture about plants named after animals. Baby spider plants dangling down from a large spider plant at least two feet across. A soft and fuzzy plant called lamb's ears and another plant, drag-on's blood, which had fleshy, blood-red leaves.

"And sanseveria, one of my favourites," said Mage Radix. "Snake plant, a real charmer, this one."

A few of the students laughed at his joke.

"Katarina has been in my family for sixty-seven years." Mage Radix ran his hand along one of the plant's leathery spiked leaves. "I inherited her from my grandmother."

Wil looked at the snake plant. It looked quite unremarkable with its silvery-green markings. But with a sudden flash of recognition, he realized that it was the same plant as the one on his grandmother's windowsill.

"We'll be learning about all the so-called animal plants," continued Mage Radix. "Then we'll turn our attention to different kinds of berries, particularly the poisonous ones, and we'll probably end off with a project on pesky plant pests and how to deal with them," he said with a wide grin.

As Wil left the greenhouse, his arm brushed against a bristly cactus and he broke out immediately in a nasty rash. Mage Radix took one look at Wil's arm and declared, "Good case of carbunculosius. It's off to the infirmary and Master Meninx for you. I'll take care of the damage here," he said, lovingly stroking the cactus, which now seemed completely harmless. "The infirmary is near Gruffud's office, down the corridor from Stone Hall. Sylvain, why don't you go with Wil?"

Sylvain grunted and stepped on the back of Wil's heel, but Wil hardly noticed as his arm felt as if it were on fire.

"Poor waddle Willy," said Sygnithia, as Wil made his way out of the greenhouse. "What's wrong? Did the itsy bitsy plant bite your hand? Sylvain, make sure the little boy doesn't get lost."

The infirmary door was closed, with a sign on it that read *Master E. Meninx.* Wil knocked while Sylvain stood behind him and snickered. When there was no answer, Wil hesitated and then opened the door quietly.

The infirmary was a long white room lined in hundreds of odd-shaped flasks, each one filled with lumpy powder or murky liquid clotted with strange bits of plant and animal floating in it. Wil's nose wrinkled at a sharp smell—it smelled like a combination of ammonia and vinegar.

Master Meninx—a small man with a wizened face and a fringed circlet of brown hair on an otherwise quite bald head—was bent over a gigantic dead fish, which was sprawled on a white table. The fish had long, bristly whiskers and seemed to be grinning at Wil.

"Um," Wil cleared his throat uncertainly, for Master Meninx had apparently still not heard him.

"Ah, excuse me, sir, I'm here to have my arm taken care of," he said.

Master Meninx looked up from the fish, his eyes unfocused at first. "Yes, may I help you?"

When Wil held out his arm, Master Meninx inspected it intently. He glanced at Sylvain, who was standing by the door and smirking. Master Meninx's thin lips pursed.

"Tsk, tsk—carbunculosis—one of Mage Radix's cactuses, I see. Nothing to smile about, Mr. Sly. Painful, carbunculosis, but easily taken care of."

Master Meninx pulled down a jar of thick, yellow ointment from one of the shelves—it smelled sweet like honey—and smeared some over the rash. To Wil's amazement, the rash disappeared almost immediately.

"Back to the greenhouse, both of you," said Master Meninx, and he returned to the dead fish without saying another word.

———

By mid-afternoon, Wil was quite sure he could not stuff anything more into his head. Everyone filed out of the greenhouse, and Wil gulped a breath of fresh, cool air.

Sygnithia and Sylvain pushed past him, both of them muttering, "Did you see he actually named one of those stupid plants?"

Wil had to admit he couldn't have agreed more.

The last class was held out behind the school in Thistleburn Field near the river. The morning rain had long since departed and the afternoon sun was relentless. Mage Quartz, the man with the three-braided beard and serpent tattoo, was the gamesmaster. He strode up and down the line of students, coaxing everyone into place. Although he was barely taller than many of the students, his voice boomed out over the playing field.

"Right. Line up, if you would please, one after the other. That's right. Just a little warm-up."

Wil wiped a rivulet of sweat from his cheek. As if we need a warm-up, he thought.

"One after the other, there you go," said Mage Quartz. "Hold on to the person in front of you. Great, great. You all know how to snake-dance, right? I'm the head of the snake. Hang on, and don't let the snake's back break!"

Wil had never heard of snake-dancing. Following everyone else, he put his hands around the waist of Olin Cramer, who was standing in front of him.

"Right—SNAKE!" shouted Mage Quartz.

Olin began to run, and Wil stumbled, but quickly recovered himself. Mage Quartz, his robes flapping behind him, ran in a great spiral circle that got tighter and tighter, until the line was so tightly coiled that Wil could scarcely breathe. Then Mage Quartz reversed direction and led them out across the field. As he was at the very end, Wil could see the long line ahead him, which really did look like some huge, undulating snake...until they all collapsed on top of each other.

Mage Quartz, his robes still flapping behind him, strode up. He pulled at his beard braids. "Great...great! Got your breath?"

Everyone was still struggling to get to their feet.

Mage Quartz rubbed his hands together and said enthusiastically, "Right, one long row please, with your backs to the sun. Follow the line of the river there. Lots of space, plenty of room—mind no one's shadow touches anyone else's."

Sylvain elbowed Wil. "Get off my shadow," he said.

"You don't need to push," said Wil.

"No arguing, boys," Mage Quartz shouted, "Right, now everyone look inside your shadow!"

Wil dutifully looked down at his shadow. The humid afternoon heat made him feel groggy and stupid, and his eyes were burning from the bright sun. His shadow looked lumpy and shapeless as usual. He looked back at Mage Quartz who was standing right behind him, and saw the serpent tattoo peeping out from under his sleeve.

"Gaze into the dark part of your shadow...*AD-UM-BRO*." Mage Quartz's voice bellowed across the field.

Wil tore his eyes from the serpent tattoo, and stared once more into his shadow.

He had the strangest sensation of separating from himself. As if standing far off, he saw himself at the edge of a high cliff. The dark shadows and shards of rock below seemed to pull at him. Dizzy, he stepped back from the edge. For a moment—one brief moment—he felt as if something were tugging away from his feet.

"Shadow-cutting. This is your first lesson for sciamachy—more colloquially known as snapdragon—one of the oldest and greatest games ever invented before serpent's time. A battle of wits between shadows!"

Wil looked back down at his shadow and was reassured to see it still firmly attached to his feet.

———cn———

Wil waited by the entrance to Stone Hall for Sophie, his head aching. Sophie hove into sight clasping a notice to her chest.

"Look what's been posted—auditions for the annual shadow play," she said excitedly. "It says *No Experience Necessary*." Her voice fell, as she read the notice. "Oh—not until the new year, way after Winterlude games in December. That's so far off." She glanced down at Wil's shoes. "Do you know your shoes still really stink?"

Before Wil could answer, he heard a woman's voice above his head.

"Shadows deceive, Portius."

Wil and Sophie both looked up at the same time to see the two heads on the stone column arguing.

"My dear Portia, on the contrary, shadows reveal material essence," said the bearded head in a deep voice. "Even with the invisibility charm, the shadow can always be seen."

"Shadows are not always what they seem, Portius," said the other head with the woman's voice. "And what are the both of you staring at?" the head said, looking down at Wil and Sophie.

"Perhaps if we introduce ourselves, Portia," said the bearded head.

"Ah yes, these are newcomers," said the first head, which bowed courteously. "I am Portia." Turning to the other head, Portia said, "And this is Portius."

"Pleased to meet you—and you," stammered Wil. He was about to hold out his hand to shake—but stopped himself short.

Instead, he asked, "Do you guard the entrance?" Then he looked at Sophie, who was laughing at him.

"We are the Gatekeeper," said the two heads in unison.

When they got outside, Wil splashed through a large puddle and turned to Sophie, "Portia and Portius, they can't keep anyone out if—if they don't have arms or legs. I mean, they can't really move, can they?"

# XVI Wil's Letter

*What if we all had two heads?*

---

*SERPENTES NUMQUAM MALI SUNT, SED RES HUMANAE SAEPE.*

SNAKES ARE NEVER EVIL, BUT OFTEN, HUMAN DEEDS ARE.

---

It was already nearing the end of September. The first month of school was almost over, and they would be visiting the snakes of Narcisse soon. Long ribbons of geese had begun flying south, the nights were cool and a few yellowed leaves were falling from trees. One night, Wil was sitting at the kitchen table beside Sophie while she did her homework. He had already finished his, so he began to write a letter to Mr. Bertram.

*Half Moon Lane, MiddleGate*

*September 26*

*Dear Mr. Bertram:*

*You would never guess what happened to Esme. She decided to explore the train and everyone was shouting and trying to catch her but she didn't want to be caught. And then I was stuck in the washroom but everything had a happy ending. I have my own bedroom here. Everybody is nice, but I think Aunt Rue is sad. Her brother disappeared ten years ago and she lights a candle for him every night.*

He looked up from the letter. "Do you think your parents will ever come back? I mean, do you think they're even alive?"

"Hmmm?" asked Sophie, putting away *Magykal Spelling, Grammar and Palaver* and pulling out her numeristics notebook.

"Do you think your parents are still alive?" Wil repeated.

"I don't know," said Sophie impatiently, as if she wanted to change the subject as quickly as possible. "Anyway, did you read about incantations? The part about repeating spells was really interesting, wasn't it?"

"Oh no, I forgot about that chapter," said Wil. He set aside the letter to Mr. Bertram, and shuffled through his books for *Magykal Spelling, Grammar and Palaver*. When he'd finished reading about repeating spells—the powerful ones only worked if said three times—he turned to his speech about the history of Gruffud's. Even though it wasn't due for weeks and weeks, until the middle of November, Sophie had already completed hers and was practising in front of the mirror after school.

———∿———

It was ten o'clock before Wil finished memorizing the week's spelling, the night before the trip to the Narcisse snakepits. "Finally," he said, throwing the list onto the floor under his bed. He looked over at Esme in her cage, but she was completely hidden except for the tip of her tail.

He pulled out the letter to Mr. Bertram, which he'd started almost a week ago, read over what he'd already written and then pulled out a pencil.

> *There are two stone heads, actually I guess they are one head, but they've got two faces, their names are Portia and Portius, at the school it's called Gruffud's Academy or Gruffud's for short. It's a school for magic. Gran always says there's no such thing as magic but some people here spell it magyk, but she must not know about Gruffud's. I know she doesn't like magic, but they don't use wands here. It's all special words, and I'm learning how to do incantations. Portia and Portius guard the school they know everything that's going on.*
>
> *The library has way more books even than you do. Peeping Peerslie lives in the library. He's a real ghost and likes to pull the books off the shelves. He helps me with my homework, but sometimes it would be easier if he didn't. Miss Heese is the*

*librarian. I really like her. Even though she goes on and on about all the library RULES, she's amazing she's helpful. She found a good article about snake eggeaters. Do you know they found a snake with two heads? I wonder if the heads can both eat eggs at the same time. There is an amazing egg shop here, where I lots of fresh eggs for Esme. The man who runs the shop, only he calls it a musée, is Mr. Egberteen. His head looks like an egg, and always giving extra eggs to Aunt Rue.*

*We are going to Narcise to see the snakes tomorrow. They hiburnate in the caves for eight months without eating. Olin says his grandfather says the snakes can hypnoties you and you forget everything you ever knew. Even if that isn't true, snakes are like creatures from another world that's the feeling I get from Esme.*

*Miss Heese showed us a newspaper article that people tried to fill the snake holes with tar and wood to burn and smoke the snakes out because they are evile, I mean they thought the snakes are evile. And snake pickers used to steal hundreds and thousands of snakes for experaments. But they aren't allowed to do that any more. If they meet Esme, I bet they will not think snakes are evile. But there was a big article in the newspaper here about the snake murders a few weeks ago that Sophie showed me, but nothing else has happened. Crows like to eat snake livers, but I don't think that is the reason so many snakes died.*

Wil bit on his pencil and wondered whether he should tell Mr. Bertram about the blue egg. Best not, he concluded.

*I hope that you are having a good time.*

*Yours sincerely,*

*Wil*

# XVII Narcisse

*Whose tracks are these?*

---

*LINGUA IPSAM VITAM HABET.*

A TONGUE HAS A LIFE OF ITS OWN.

---

It was one of those sweltering September days—summer heat's last gasp. Mage Adderson and Miss Heese were chatting with the bus driver about which route to take to Narcisse.

"Mr. Wychwood, very good," said a flushed Mage Terpsy, and she crossed Wil's name off her list as he boarded the bus for Narcisse.

As Sophie was already sitting with Merrily Klimchak, Wil sat beside Jinzhen Cheng, who was talking with his friends in the seat behind.

A long limousine drew up beside the bus in a cloud of dust, and a hubbub broke out.

"It's the Minister." "What's he doing here?" "I'd love a ride in that thing!"

The chauffeur opened the rear door and the short man with black shoe-polish hair, whom Wil had seen in Pirsstle and Bertram's—and then at the train station—climbed out and strode to the bus.

"Minister Skelch, we are so honoured!" exclaimed Mage Terpsy. "Skinister Melch is responsible, children, for enforcing legislation to protect the snakes and their habitat."

Minister Skelch smiled benevolently, apparently ignoring the fact that Mage Terpsy had just mangled his name. "Thank you, Mage Terpsy," he said, wheezing. "Sorry—only just able to get away. Mind if I join you? You know that you youngsters are the Future Guardians of Narcisse."

———ɔⅼɔ———

At last, the bus pulled out from the school grounds. Wil should have been excited about seeing the snakes. But he now had a slight headache from everyone's chatter. Jostled by the bus, he closed his eyes and began to doze.

In a dreamlike state, he saw flames licking up the third floor window-sill above the Japanese restaurant. The snake plant on the windowsill was waving in slow motion. Then, as if replaying a movie, he saw something he hadn't seen before...someone staggering away from the back of the building. Who was it?

A man, a short man with black hair—and he reminded Wil of Minister Skelch.

The bus lurched to a sudden stop. Wil opened his eyes and stared at the Minister, who was laughing loudly. Sweat trickled down Wil's back and he felt sick.

He looked out the window in time to see the bus driver inserting an ornate key into a hole in a stone wall. The driver returned to his seat, and the bus jolted forward and lurched over two bumps into a tunnel lit by lanterns. It was the same way they had entered MiddleGate. Wil was sure they would smash into the end of the tunnel, but suddenly the wall began to blur and turned into the mural of the *Black Mirror* chocolates. There was the house with the five-pointed stars again. This time, Wil noticed carvings at the top of the house that looked like snakes curling around each other.

He turned to Jinzhen. "How did we do that?" he asked.

"Do what?"

"You know—go through that wall? And what's the house with the stars?"

It was obvious from Jinzhen's face that Wil's question was silly.

"That's the gate," said Jinzhen.

Wil must have looked puzzled, because Jinzhen repeated, "It's a gate. MiddleGate is like—" He paused. "—like a pocket ...a big pocket inside the city...it's secret."

"Oh, a secret city; but how come no one knows about it?"

"There's a repel charm."

"Are there other places like MiddleGate?"

But Jinzhen had already turned back to talking with his friends, and didn't answer.

———ch———

The bus barrelled along the open road. Pastures gave way to flat fields of rippling wheat, and bales of hay—huge, round biscuits—dotted the horizon. As they drove farther north, abandoned houses and swayback barns were sinking into wild grasses, gravestones leaned perilously in derelict cemeteries, and exploded tire shreds pitched like so many dead blackbirds along the highway. The black and white flash of a magpie landed on a small pyramid of stones in a field spotted with hundreds of boulders, and the bus passed a small sign by the roadside—Mosquito Ranch.

Wil heard the shouts long before the bus turned into the parking lot. More than twenty people with placards were marching across the entranceway: *Ban Snakeseers. Serpicide! Serpicide! S.O.S. Save Our Snakes. Save Our Snakes. Save Our Snakes!"*

The bus stopped and one of the protesters mounted the steps of bus. Although Wil couldn't hear what Mage Adderson said, the man directed the throng to let the bus pass. One of the protesters, his face painted in green and yellow stripes, shouted at them as they passed through the line of placards; his tongue was swollen and pink. Thinking of Esme's delicate snout and dainty tongue, Wil recoiled.

"Could I have everyone's attention please," said Mage Adderson in a loud voice, "before we disembark from the bus. Remain together— no wandering off from the trail and getting lost. This is a sacred site—no shouting or shrieking, and no games of tag or hide-and-go-seek. We will have our picnic near the fourth snakepit. And I believe Mage Terpsy is expecting a brief essay—as part of your language arts studies in verbology—on your observations of the snakes and their habitat, are you not, Mage Terpsy?"

Mage Terpsy beamed at everyone.

The afternoon heat hit Wil's face as he dismounted from the bus. The sky was turning cloudy and Wil tasted hot dust in the air. A woman in a bright yellow uniform was handing out pamphlets while she talked to a small group of a dozen people.

"We have many school tours," said the woman in the yellow uniform. "Several hundred students visit sometimes and I have to stand on a picnic table so everyone can hear me. Now, one of you was asking about those little highway fences; they guide the snakes to tunnels underneath the road. Ten thousand snakes a year were lost before those fences and tunnels were installed. Horrific mortality rate."

The thought of ten thousand snakes dead made Wil feel more ill than ever.

"A good thing for the snakes with so many people here, even though some believe otherwise." The woman in the yellow uniform pointed to the protesters at the entranceway. "They all help keep the crows away." The woman took off her hat and wiped her brow. "Some children are forced on to the bus. At the first hibernaculum—that's a big word for a little snake den—they're squeamish; they won't even look at the snakes. The second one—they're touching the snakes. By the third den, they're holding the snakes!"

# XVIII Lost

*What is the difference between a maze and a labyrinth?*

---

*SERPENTES VEL HOMINES—PARITER DIGNA SCRUTARI.*
TO OBSERVE THE SNAKES OR TO OBSERVE THE HUMANS—
BOTH WORTHY PURSUITS.

---

Sophie didn't stop to listen to the woman in the yellow uniform. Instead, she followed Mage Terpsy and Miss Heese, who were walking with several other students.

The aspen woods were small and stunted. Only a few gnarled old oak trees pushed skyward. Roots and jutting stones threatened her every step.

"Why don't you folks back it up," shouted a man's voice ahead on the trail.

Sophie rounded the corner, almost running into the lens of a television camera.

"Yikes!" said the man's voice. "Here you go, little girl. Careful there."

Sophie was hoisted up by the back of her shirt, and she found herself looking into the pockmarked face of a man holding a camera.

"Would you mind moving out of the way, little girl? We're in the middle of a shoot," said the man.

Sophie trudged on ahead, muttering to herself, "I am not a *little girl*." She turned to look around at the crew filming two women and a man strolling along the trail. Having fallen behind the others, Sophie was now alone. She broke into a trot to catch up, but there were so many stones on the path, that she fell again and found herself face to face with a small, slender snake. It stared at her for a long moment, flicking its tongue—just like Esme did.

Sophie felt hypnotized, unable to move. She heard hissing in her ears, as if hundreds of snakes were singing. The snake turned its head slowly, deliberately, and then slithered off into the woods. The hissing sound dwindled and then was gone.

———⌇———

Wil walked slowly to the first snakepit. Bright green moss covered the sinkhole, and Wil caught a glimpse of dozens of snakes gliding towards the entrance. There were only a couple of other students from Gruffud's at the den—the rest must have gone ahead already. He found himself standing behind a mother who was waving her toddler's hand at the snakes.

"Bye-bye, bye-bye, snakie," said the mother in a high, singsong voice.

The toddler, though, was plainly more interested in chewing on the red rubber snake he was holding.

A camera crew was filming two women and a man, while a man in a yellow uniform stood close by. One of the women, who was wearing dangly earrings and high-heeled shoes, was holding a snake. The man, his shaved head glistening in the sun, held out his finger to touch the snake. His face looked like he had just bitten into a sour lemon. The crew moved in for a close-up shot of his finger on the snake's scales.

"It's like silk, like satin sheets, isn't it?" said the man with the shaved head. "I had no idea they were so soft. Not so close, not so close," he squealed, sounding slightly hysterical.

"Hey, we're losing the sound," said one of the crew. "Bring the mikes over here."

"Yuck, it peed on me!" screeched the dangly earrings woman, and she dropped the snake on the ground.

"Cut!" yelled the cameraman.

The snake slithered away.

"Use two hands; don't let it dangle," said the man in the yellow uniform. "Let it go—easy, easy, from one hand to another, just like a Slinky. Remember, these snakes are not venomous."

Disappointed that he wasn't able to get closer to the snakes, Wil continued along a path that opened up into an enormous field of yellow grasses. Way off in the distance, he saw the silhouette of large crow swaying at the top of a tree. He walked past a collapsed sinkhole overgrown with long grasses. At least a dozen snakes, all of them dead, were scattered around the rock outcropping.

The rotting smell of death was overwhelming—he felt like retching—but Wil knelt down beside one of the longer snakes. It must have been female. They were bigger than the males, he'd heard the woman in the yellow uniform say. The snake was perfect in death as in life. He poked at the snake with a stick, and lifted it up. It dangled limply, and pale white maggots wriggled out of the corpse, apparently frantic to escape the hot sun. Wil dropped the stick and the snake. Feeling heartsick, he picked up another stick and moulded the body of the snake into a spiral shape, as if it were sleeping.

He poked at another snake body, this one dried and mummified in the sun. Its tiny backbones were bleached white. Wil pulled out the bones one by one, pocketed them, and then walked on slowly, pausing to look at a boulder covered in lichens and a tall, twisted oak tree beside the trail—it was the only tall tree for miles.

Hundreds of snakes were rustling amidst dried leaves and brown vines at the second den. There were a few Gruffud's students milling about here, but Wil still didn't see Sophie. Broken glass spilled out of a paper bag someone had tossed on the rocks. A couple of pop bottles and cigarette butts were also scattered amidst the rocks, along with an old faded pink handkerchief. Why would people drop their garbage, and who would drop a handkerchief anyway? Wil saw his own long shadow on the rocks below. The rotting stench of a dead snake assailed his nostrils—another snake had been punctured and left to die. He turned away, reminded of Esme.

The camera crew had caught up, and Wil overheard the dangly earrings woman saying, "I remember when I was little— but you know, we manifest fears we never had when we were kids. A year ago, I would have had a nervous breakdown, if you'd told me I'd be walking around with a snake in my hand."

"I'll never forget the little white snake wriggling out of a crate of mangoes," said the man with the shaved head. "I was six years old—but it's time to move on now." His voice sounded shaky.

The second woman, dressed in a shocking pink sun hat, seemed to be reassuring the dangly earrings woman and the man with the shaved head. "You're both doing so well. Ophidiophobia—fear of snakes—can cripple some people emotionally." Then she smiled brightly and said, "Would you like to tell the television audience how you feel? And will you come here again?"

Wil overheard a man in a yellow uniform talking in a low voice to one of the sightseers. "They had to have special permission to film, you know. That woman over there, the one in the pink hat—she's a therapist—been working with the other two for a year. They were mortally afraid of snakes. Oh, we get film crews from all over coming here, from Israel, France, Germany, England—all over. Last year a crew from Thailand piled the snakes on top of the TV host!"

Wil stood watching the crew, which was taking advantage of the afternoon's lengthening shadows to film the second woman holding another snake. The man obviously didn't want to touch the snake this time. The anchorman zeroed in on the writhing shadow of the snake on the dusty ground.

Wil left the camera crew behind and set off for the third den. He saw Sophie walking alone way ahead.

"Sophie, Sophie, wait up," he shouted.

She turned around and waved.

Breathless, and holding the chain around his neck so it wouldn't swing about too much, Wil caught up with her.

"I've been thinking about those snakes that were killed. Whoever would do that..." Wil's voice trailed off. "You know, I bet it isn't really the crows." He scratched his leg and shooed away a couple of mosquitoes.

"Well, if it's not the crows, what could it be?" asked Sophie.

"I don't know."

"Shouldn't we be at the third den soon?" said Sophie. She pulled out a map.

"Where did you get that map?"

"They were at the entranceway." Sophie pointed to the map. "I think we're right here."

Sophie folded the map up and put it back in her pocket. "We'll go this way."

But the trees all looked the same, their black and white bark glinting in the late afternoon sun. At the end of several more minutes tromping through the underbrush, Wil and Sophie looked at each other and then burst out laughing because each of them had leaves and twigs stuck in their hair.

"You look like a real mess," said Wil.

"Pull your own nose," retorted Sophie.

"What's that supposed to mean?"

"It means you don't look any better!"

Wil cupped his hands and tried to throw his voice as far as he could. "Hello. Can anyone hear us? Hello—we're over here."

A cicada answered them with a high-pitched buzz.

They called until they were hoarse.

"Bet Sygnithia and Sylvain wouldn't help even if they did hear us calling," said Wil. "Why are they always so rude, anyway?"

"It's not you," said Sophie, pulling burrs out of her hair.

"What do you mean, it's not me?"

"They just don't like our family."

"Why not? Is that why you don't have any friends?"

"I don't know what you're talking about," said Sophie, her voice rising up a notch. "Anyway, I don't need any friends."

The frames of Sophie's eyeglasses had turned white, but Wil pressed on. "What's wrong with our family?"

"Well, if you really must know, everyone thinks that my father was a murderer. The only reason Aunt Rue still has her job at the Secretariat is because they took pity on her."

"A murderer?" repeated Wil. So I come from a family of murderers after all, he thought. "Did he kill someone?"

Sophie yanked a branch out her hair. "Do you have to keep repeating it?"

"Don't you think I ought to know what kind of family I come from— as if I had any choice."

"Fine then, if that's how you feel," said Sophie. "You didn't have to come and live with us."

"It would be nice if I knew what everyone is saying," said Wil, almost crashing into a tree trunk. "I'm sick of Sygnithia and Sylvain calling me names."

Sophie stopped to rest against a tree and fingered its smooth, white bark. She looked resigned. "Okay, but I don't know the whole story. Aunt Rue and Aunt Violet always look as if they're going to cry whenever I ask them about it.

"My father was working late one night in the library. He returned home, delirious, muttering about having fallen and hit his head. The librarian was found dead the next day—in the library. My father was apparently the only witness—even Peeping Peerslie didn't know anything—but my father couldn't remember a thing. It was like his mind had been wiped clean. Then two days later, he just disappeared. Everyone thought he was guilty."

There was a deep rumble of thunder off in the distance. The frames of Sophie's eyeglasses had turned a nasty puce, and she looked like she about to cry. Then she gasped, pointing at his chest.

"Wil, look. The serpent on the black medallion is shining."

71

# XIX Hibernaculum

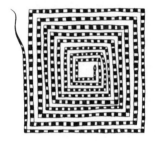

*Didn't we come this way before?*

---

*IN LABYRINTHO, AEQUO ANIMO ESTO.*
KEEP CALM IN A LABYRINTH (OR MAZE).

---

Everyone was sitting on colourful picnic blankets; mounds of egg sandwiches and pickles were disappearing quickly.

Mage Terpsy sat down on a bench and fanned herself with a notebook. "Fewer snakes this year, but perhaps the children won't notice."

Miss Heese nodded and sat down beside Mage Terpsy. "Vigilance," she said, as she mopped her brow with a handkerchief. "These sssnakes are a national treasure. Our children and our children's children will guard these snakesss. With the Order of the Snakesss demanding an inquiry, the authorities should take ssswift action."

Miss Heese smiled at Minister Skelch holding court in the midst of a large circle of students. "Minister, what do you think?" she asked.

Minister Skelch cleared his throat. "We are making every effort—no stone unturned, no crystal unpolished, as it were—to protect Narcisse, Miss Heese." He launched into a speech about The Importance of the Snakes of Narcisse to Our History, and vilified anyone who would harm them.

Sygnithia Sly tugged at Mage Terpsy's sleeve, with a grin on her face. "Yes, Miss Sly?" said Mage Terpsy, but she turned back to the Minister.

Sygnithia tugged at Mage Terpsy's sleeve again. "Wil Wychwood and Sophie Isidor are missing, Mage Terpsy."

"Well, they must be somewhere," said Mage Terpsy, looking alarmed.

Word spread. No one had seen Wil and Sophie for a long time.

"Trust those two to get lost—and wreck it for everyone else," said Sygnithia in a loud voice to Regina Piehard.

———

"Why is the black medallion glowing?" asked Sophie. "Remember when Cadmus and Esme—"

"Yeah, it was shining then too," said Wil. "We must be near the right path. The sun is there, so that's west, right?"

"I suppose so." Sophie yanked a thorn from her hair. "Stupid branches."

"This path looks well-used," he said. "Maybe it will take us back."

"Didn't we come this way before?" asked Sophie in a plaintive voice. "If we had some string—"

"Or crumbs of bread—then we could be like Hansel and Gretel," said Wil.

"Don't be snarky," said Sophie.

Wil slapped two mosquitoes. "Why did I follow you, anyway?"

"Well, *I* didn't invite you."

They continued walking, until Sophie broke the silence. "Do you have anything to eat?"

One bubblegum and four grimy peppermints—not enough to keep stomachs from growling.

"Bet they've eaten lunch by now," said Sophie, and she looked up at the looming dark grey clouds.

Thunder rumbled, closer than before.

———

Phosphoworm lanterns bobbled in the fading light, and voices echoed. "SOPHEEEE! WIL!"

Despite Mage Adderson's stern admonitions that crying would do no good, many of the children were tearful.

"Mage Terpsy shall remain here with me and we shall continue searching," said Mage Adderson. "I want the children on the bus, Miss

**73**

Heese. "All of you shall return to Gruffud's. I've sent messages to Mage Agassiz and Miss Isidor's family. And Minister Skelch—where is the Minister?"

"He must be contacting the Secretariat," said Miss Heese.

At that moment, Minister Skelch stepped out of the darkness. "Regrettable, most regrettable," he murmured.

"There you are, Minister," said Miss Heese. "Where have you been?"

Minister Skelch looked startled and hesitated before answering, "Arrangements for a search party have been made with the warden."

"They can't have gone that far," said Mage Terpsy, her voice warbling. "Do you think it would help to fight a liar, keep our spirits up?"

Mage Adderson looked puzzled for a moment. "Light a fire, do you mean?" She glanced at the heavy, glowering clouds. "I shouldn't think so."

———

Sophie shivered at a low, hooting sound. "Did you hear that?"

"Just an owl," said Wil, but Sophie noticed his voice trembled a little.

"Do you think they know we're missing?" asked Sophie.

If Wil answered, his reply was swallowed up by the crackling and rustling all around them. The rocks themselves seemed to be alive and moving. Snakes were sliding over their feet and Sophie hoped she wasn't stepping on any of them. "We're going to get soaked," she said.

"If the snakes are heading to the caves," said Wil, "there must be one nearby."

"How do you follow snakes in the dark?" asked Sophie. "Anyway, I don't want to go inside a cave where there are hundreds of snakes. Esme is a nice snake, but this is different." She watched a glint of water dangling from Wil's nose, and wondered how long it would take to fall.

"They won't eat you. These snakes won't even bite. And at least we'd be out of the rain." Wil wiped away the drop of water from his nose. "If this medallion could light up—"

Sophie gave a small shriek as a slim beam of light shot out from the snake on the medallion. "How did you do that? It just lit up all by itself!"

Now they could see several snakes slithering ahead.

"Don't know," said Wil. "Quick, follow those snakes."

Together they scrambled after the snakes, trying not to get tangled in the bushes. Groping about they found a small cavern covered in vines. Even in broad daylight, it would have been hard to see the entrance with all these vines, thought Sophie.

74

They felt their way along the rough rock until the small cavern opened into a larger cave.

Sophie's nose wrinkled at the smell of something rotting. "What a horrible, putrid smell," she said, her voice trembling. "Like something dead."

"Maybe this wasn't such a good idea after all," said Wil. "Don't step on any of the snakes."

"I'm trying not to," said Sophie, stepping gingerly. "I think I'd rather be outside. This smell—"She stopped with a choking sound.

"What's the matter?" asked Wil.

"Look at that!" Sophie said.

"What?"

"That!"

Sophie pointed to the back of the cave. There were piles of snakeskins stacked against the wall. Wil stepped over to the pile and pulled one skin out. "They're real—" he said.

The light from the medallion faded, and they were left in the dark.

"Watch out, that's my foot you're on," said Wil.

"Great idea coming in here," said Sophie. Then she gasped. "Something brushed against me!"

They both heard what sounded like dry snakeskins scattering and rattling against the floor of the cave.

"Let's get out of here," said Wil. "I don't care if it's raining."

———

Mage Adderson's chiselled features and sharp nose looked haggard by the light of the phosphoworm lanterns on the picnic tables near the parking lot. "Well, Miss Isidor and Mr. Wychwood," she said, frowning, "you are to be commended for your audacity and stupidity in striking out on your own...and for your sheer dumb luck in making your way back."

Mage Terpsy, for once, was bereft of words, and gave Sophie and Wil a hug.

Miss Heese arrived, quite breathless, waving her handkerchief in her hand. "Where in serpent's sake have you been? All the other children are on the bus."

"We tried to follow the map," said Sophie, "but we got more lost."

"Well, you're safe now. That's what's important," said Miss Heese, patting Sophie on the head.

Minister Skelch looked down at Wil's hand, and his brow furrowed. "What's that you've got there?" he asked.

"It's a snakeskin, sir," Wil said. "We found a whole stash in one of the caves."

In the shocked silence that followed, everyone looked down at the crinkled snakeskin in Wil's hand.

Mage Terpsy spoke first. "That's impossible. Snakes don't deposit their moulted skins in piles."

"But it's a real skin—I mean, I think it's a skinned skin," Wil said.

"There must be some explanation," said Miss Heese, as she inspected the snakeskin. "Don't you think so, Minister?"

Minister Skelch cleared his throat. "We mustn't jump to conclusions. The children should rest and we'll investigate things in the morning. Perhaps, Mage Adderson—although school discipline is obviously quite beyond the Secretariat's control—"

Mage Adderson bowed her head.

"—perhaps, given the important discovery the children seem to have made, their disobedience and failure to return with the others could be excused?"

Wil looked gratefully at Minister Skelch but was shocked to see that the Minister's face seemed to have aged twenty years. By the flickering light of the phosphoworms, Minister Skelch reminded Wil again of the man who had staggered away from the fire on Harbinger Street. He stepped back, certain the Minister would somehow hear what he was thinking.

"Look at you both—covered in mosssquito bites!" Miss Heese hovered over Wil and Sophie, bundling them in blankets. "Sssetting off on your own, you sssilly children."

# XX  Lies and Mud

*Would you trust a gargoyle?*

---

*CAVE MONSTRA.*

BE CAREFUL OF GARGOYLES. BE VERY CAREFUL.

"Wil, wake up," said Sophie, standing at the doorway of Wil's bedroom. "Come on, bedhead!"

"What?" mumbled Wil. He tried—unsuccessfully—to open his eyes.

"There's an article in the newspaper," said Sophie.

Wil groaned and managed to open one eye, but Sophie had already shut the door. Still wearing his pyjamas, Wil lurched down the stairs to find Sophie sitting with Aunt Rue and Aunt Violet at the breakfast table. Sophie was reading the newspaper, and she was covered in strange red circles, as if she'd contracted some incurable disease.

"What happened to you?" Wil asked.

Sophie held up a pen on which bright red letters were flashing— *Anti-SkitterJitter.* "If you draw a circle with this pen, it takes away the itching," she said.

The cure looks worse than the disease, thought Wil.

"Just draw a circle around all your mosquito bites," she said, as she held out the pen to him.

"No, thanks," said Wil, certain that the red circles would only make it easier to find the welts and scratch them.

Sophie turned back to the newspaper.

"Sophie, dear," said Aunt Violet, who was clipping spiky leaves one by one into a large pile on the table, "why don't you read the article for us. I can't seem to find my eyeglasses this morning."

"They're right under that heap of leaves, Aunt Violet," said Aunt Rue. Her scissors snapped as she cut out a coupon from *The Daily Magezine*, and added it to a stash of coupons.

Wil glanced at the coupon nearest him—

*50¢ Off*
*One-Shot No-Spot Cleaning Powder*
*Guaranteed to Leave Your Counters, Floors and Walls*
*Sparkling in No Time*

"Aunt Rue, don't you remember the last time you used One-Shot No-Spot, it ate a hole right through the floor?" asked Sophie. She grinned at Wil, and began reading in a dramatic voice:

LOST CHILDREN STUMBLE ON MUTILATED SNAKES

*Two children lost in the Narcisse snakepits last night found hundreds of snakeskins in one of the caves.*

*"It was horrible. There were thousands of them," said Sophie Isidor (daughter of the late Cyril Isidor) and her cousin William Wychwood. Both of them were on a Gruffud's Academy field trip and had strayed into one of the snake dens during a storm.*

*One of the snakeskins they found has been turned over to authorities. No other evidence of snakeskins in any of the Narcisse caves has been found, however. All precautionary checks—including reverse invisibility charms—have been conducted, to no avail.*

*Investigations into the allegations are continuing. The Secretariat on the Status of Magical Creatures has not yet issued any formal statement. SSMC Minister Skelch who happened to be accompanying the field trip at the time has stated: "We mustn't jump to any conclusions. One cannot always rely upon on children's stories."*

*That leaves the nagging question—just what did the children see? [Report by Reece Rebus]*

"He's calling us liars!" said Wil, now fully awake.

"I would hope not, my dears," said Aunt Violet. She was expecting the ladies from the MiddleGate Horticultural Society on their annual autumn tour later that afternoon, and was now fussing over ribbons and small bundles of dried leaves on the kitchen table. "You can't believe half of what you read in the newspaper," she said, as she twisted a blue ribbon. "But we know you saw the snakeskins."

"Sophie, why don't you and Wil water Aunt Violet's garden before the ladies come so everything is fresh," said Aunt Rue. "Mind you don't get your father's gargoyle wet."

Sophie and Wil stepped out into the back garden, which was crammed with so many flowers and shrubs that it was hard to move. A narrow brick path wended through the greenery. Plump grapes dangling above their heads had begun turning a mouth-watering purple. Wil picked up one of the watering cans, which was already full to the brim, and followed Sophie along the path.

"Sophie, remember when Minister Skelch told Adderson to go easy on us?" asked Wil. "Because we'd discovered something important?"

"Yes," replied Sophie, turning around to look at Wil.

"I think it's the Minister."

"What do you mean?" said Sophie, staring at Wil.

"He looks like the man I saw running from the fire when my grandmother died—a short man with black hair. Maybe he's the one who murdered the snakes."

"What are you talking about? He's the *Minister*," Sophie hissed. "Remember I told you about the Secretariat—where my mother works?"

"Well," said Wil, "maybe it is ridiculous, but the Minister was in Pirsstle and Bertram's, the bookstore where I used to work, and that was the day before the fire. Then he was at the train station. I overheard him say, 'Time is of the essence.' That's because the snakes would be returning to their caves and hibernating soon, right?"

Sophie rolled her eyes. "Wil, you're crazy. He's the Minister, for serpent's sake!" Sophie's eyeglass frames turned from light yellow to vivid pink. "And what's all this got to do with your grandmother dying in that fire? Don't water the chocolate mint too much, and be careful of the gargoyle."

Wil was staying as far away from the stone gargoyle as possible. He'd seen garden ornaments before—gnomes holding rakes, frogs with bulging eyes and puckered lips spouting water or plastic geese lined up in a row. Although those looked alive from a distance, they weren't—not like the gargoyle. It was an ill-tempered creature, and for some reason, it detested getting wet. Its snout wrinkled whenever Wil approached. At the moment, the gargoyle was baring its sharp teeth, and its bulbous eyes were looking at him sideways in a most unpleasant way.

When he didn't answer Sophie, her voice grew shriller. "You can't go around saying that the Minister murdered the snakes when you have no proof. Besides, it's the Minister's job to protect the snakes, not kill them!" The frames of Sophie's eyeglasses were now turning orange streaked with red.

"You think we imagined all those snakeskins?" asked Wil hotly. He glanced again at the gargoyle and noticed its spiral tail was starting to unwind.

"No, we didn't," said Sophie. But she sounded doubtful. "Look, you almost got the gargoyle's tail wet! Watch what you're doing."

"What does that old gargoyle do when it rains anyway?"

"Rain is different," said Sophie. "Last time someone splashed water—"

But Sophie didn't have a chance to tell what happened last time, because Wil tripped over a stone and water splashed the gargoyle.

Before Wil was able to duck, the gargoyle hurled a sticky clot of mud at him, which struck him right on the nose. Wil tried to dodge the next missile, but the gargoyle pelted him with all the mud balls it could muster. Its claws scratched at the ground, flinging Aunt Violet's herbs in all directions. The long tail whipped from side to side. The creature was in such a fury that Wil was soon covered head to toe in mud

"You're ruining Aunt Violet's garden," shrieked Sophie. "You're not supposed to get the gargoyle wet—especially its tail."

"Me? *I'm* going to ruin the garden? What about that thing?" panted Wil as he pointed at the gargoyle.

But the gargoyle was crouching on its haunches, its long tail coiled in a perfect, innocent spiral.

All around, a hurricane seemed to have struck. Plants lay strewn about, their roots exposed. Bruised flower petals were scattered everywhere.

Wil's pyjamas were soggy, and his toes squelched with each step. He wiped the mud dripping from his nose.

"If you had concentrated on watering, and not gone on about the Minister being a murderer—" Sophie said. She stopped, a look of fright on her face.

Wil turned his head and saw Aunt Violet at the back door. She was scowling at Wil more ferociously than the gargoyle had.

# XXI Two-Headed Dog

*What if you had a snake's tail?*

---

*NEMPE DUO ETIAM TRIA CAPITA MELIORA QUAM UNUM SUNT.*
SURELY TWO—OR EVEN THREE—HEADS ARE BETTER THAN ONE.

---

Wil and Sophie were famous around the school for two whole weeks after the Narcisse field trip—despite Sygnithia and Sylvain's taunts.

"Oh, the famous cave explorers—please, Lady Soppy and Sir Willmore Worthless, may I have your autographs?" said Sylvain one day before verbology class, while Sygnithia pranced about pretended to pose for a photograph. "Enjoy your moment of glory in the limelight," sneered Sylvain. "Soon, you'll be back to no friends."

"You're just jealous, you two," said Sophie.

"Yeah, is that all you can come up with?" added Wil. Willmore Worthless was just another one of Sylvain's names for Wil. Willy, Willard, Windle, Wilston, Wilbur, Wilton...Waldo...Willus—Wil had stopped keeping track after a while.

———⌁———

The snakes of Narcisse were hibernating now and their murders were all but forgotten. And, just as Sylvain had predicted, Wil and Sophie had returned to relative obscurity.

It was the end of October, and everyone at Gruffud's was busy preparing for the Halloween Masquerade Ball. They had spent the last two days carving dozens of the huge pumpkins that Mage Radix had grown, and the air in the school was filled with a rich, earthy smell.

The night of Halloween was cold and clear. The leering pumpkin lanterns lined Stone Hall, and black candles floating in mid-air cast eerie shadows. The whole hall smelled like pumpkin pie.

Wil was shocked to see blue flames flicker across Portia's and Portius's faces, as if they were wearing veils of fire.

A lick of blue flame curled from Portia's mouth as she exclaimed, "Look at Mage Terpsy!"

Mage Terpsy was a walking portrait dressed in a flouncy dress with massive pink bows and an ornate gilded frame. Her arms protruded from the painting, as did her round face. The frame was so wide that she kept bumping into everyone and apologizing profusely each time.

"Now I wonder who that is over there," said Portius, "with the missing head. Alas, Mage Terpsy is blocking the way. Portia, my dear, can you see?"

"Missing head, did you say?" Portia strained her neck so far out that Wil was sure her own head was in danger of falling onto the floor below.

Wil recognized the person with the missing head immediately from the serpent tattoo on his left hand. It was Mage Quartz and his neck—or where his neck should have been—was oozing red paint. At least, Wil hoped it was just paint, for the dribbles did look very real. Mage Quartz's eyes glinted through two small holes cut in the cloth neck and he was holding a severed head with two glass eyes.

Wil sympathized with Portia and Portius, who shrank from the gruesome sight of that poor head separated from its own neck. Both of them cringed until just the tips of their noses were visible, and sparks flickered from their nostrils.

Portia and Portius recovered themselves quickly, however, at the sight of an intruder.

"No, no. We regret to inform you—" said Portius.

"—that you cannot pass this place," said Portia.

"Disguised, you may enter."

"All others, turn aside."

Wil peeped around the column. Portia's and Portius's serpent braids had begun to slide down the column towards Minister Skelch...who was costumeless. Wil swallowed hard, and his heart began pounding.

Just at that moment, Mage Terpsy bustled up in her portrait frame. "Oh, Skinister Melch, wonderful to see you," she said breathlessly. "Portia and Portius, may I introduce you. This is our new Minister of the Secretariat on the Status of Magical Creatures, a former student of Gruffud's, as you no doubt remember."

"Thank you, Mage Terpsy," said Minister Skelch. He bowed low. "Portia and Portius, ever-faithful Gatekeeper, what would Gruffud's be without you?"

Portia and Portius, however, were not to be placated. Only when Minister Skelch opened his cape and revealed a skeleton costume underneath—and then pulled a skull mask from his pocket—did Portia and Portius allow him past the entranceway. Both heads were still grumbling as the snake braids returned to their usual length.

"Fancy trying to get in without a costume," said Portius.

"The nerve—" said Portia, the blue flames on her face flaring for an instant.

"Even if he is Minister—" said Portius.

"—he ought to know!" snapped Portia. "Not all that long ago that Erro Skelch was a student here himself—could never be quite sure what that boy was thinking about."

The revelation increased Wil's distrust of Minister Skelch, but these thoughts were interrupted by his name being called.

"...been looking for you everywhere, Wil," said Sophie in a muffled voice. She was wearing the head of a black dog with a large snout and sharp white teeth. A second dog's head dangled from the heavy cloak she was wearing.

"Sorry. I've been right here all along," Wil said. He slipped under the cloak, and put on the second head...it was hot and stuffy inside.

The moth-eaten costume had been in Aunt Violet's closet for years. It smelled of cedar chips and reminded Wil of his grandmother's clothes closet. Originally, there had been three heads, but the third one had lost most of its fur, so Aunt Violet took it off and sewed the cloak up. Even though he and Sophie had practised for hours around the house, it was still awkward walking together. Tonight, the fake fur was unbearably itchy.

"You're on my foot," said Sophie, sounding testy.

"It's hard to see from in here," said Wil, tugging at the nose of his dog's head. "Do you know what I just found out?"

"What?" asked Sophie.

"Minister Skelch used to be a student here at Gruffud's, and Portia and Portius said—"

"So, lots of people have gone to Gruffud's," said Sophie. "What's so special about that?"

"Yeah, I guess you're right," said Wil and he forgot what he was going to say next, for Portius was whispering something to Portia.

"That creature looks familiar, doesn't it, Portia? Yes, but there were three heads, as I remember."

"Yes, three friends—one no longer with us, or so it is supposed," said Portia.

"Hush, Portia, or the children will hear you."

Before Wil could ask Portia and Portius what they were talking about, Portius turned to Wil and Sophie and said in a hearty voice. "Fair heads, Mr. Wychwood and Miss Isidor. A pity so few people have more than one head. How do you manage?"

Portia and Portius began to bicker about the virtues of having one head or two. Despite differences on minor points, they seemed to agree that anyone with only one head must be operating at a distinct disadvantage.

Wil and Sophie left them in the middle of their discussion and stumbled together over to the table of sweets. The table was laden with mounds of snakecake, jellywobbles, sugared grapes, honeyed lemonpops, chocolate toads, and zebra whirls. Wil reached for snakecake—his favourite—a rich, striped wafer, topped with shimmering, candied scales. As he leaned over the table, his furry dog's head toppled right into a large bowl of whipped cream.

Sophie laughed so loudly that her own dog's head almost fell off, and everyone crowded around to see what the matter was.

"You're frothing at the mouth, Wychwood!" said Sylvain who was wearing a gold crown and blue velvet cape.

Master Meninx—dressed as a spider with eight wobbling, hairy arms—hurried up at all the commotion. "What in snake's sake!" he exclaimed.

## XXII Alas, Poor Portia

*Who was it?*

---

*SEMPER PEIUS SIT.*

IT COULD ALWAYS BE WORSE.

---

Master Meninx deftly undid the snaps holding Wil's dog's head to the cloak. "Why don't you go to the washroom and wash the whipped cream off, Mr. Wychwood," he said, stepping back from Wil in distaste, as some of the cream dripped onto one of his spider legs.

Feeling as if everyone were laughing at him, Wil pushed his way past the lineup for the costume parade, and finally made it to the washroom. As he opened the door, a great glop of cream splat on the floor, and then he heard a menacing voice say, "Don't be naive. Your position won't protect you."

Wil froze for a moment, stepped backwards, slipped on the glop of cream...and fell to the bathroom floor. What he saw was terrifying. He closed his eyes, hoping that when he opened them, the bathroom would be as it always was—with spotless mirrors and gleaming black and white tiles.

He opened his eyes, and the same terrible sight greeted him.

Two masqueraders—both dressed as skeletons—were wrestling with each other. One of the skull masks had slipped so now it appeared to have two mouths—one fleshy-pink, the other, cadaver-grey.

"Sorr-eeeee," Wil stuttered and he struggled to right himself.

The skeletons turned at the sound of his voice. Before Wil even had time to think, they pulled him to his feet without a word and propped the dripping dog's head on a wooden chair in the corner of the washroom. Then they left the room so quickly, Wil thought he had imagined it all.

Dazed, he watched a large butterfly wing poke through the doorway, then a second wing, followed in short order by Mrs. Pyper with a pair of sparkling antennae waggling on her head.

"Mage Agassiz told me you were in a spot of trouble, my dear!" Mrs. Pyper laughed, and the butterfly wings jiggled up and down.

"A little soggy," she said, as she washed off the dog's head. "But there you go. That ought to do it." She scrubbed the cream from the back of Wil's cloak, dabbed his chin and with a waggle of her antennae, clapped him on the back. "Now you go and have a good time with your friends."

"Thank you, Mrs. Pyper," said Wil. He left her scrubbing so furiously, he thought she would wear a hole in the floor.

He found Sophie near the entrance to Stone Hall, her dog's head dangling down her back. "Wait until you hear—" he said.

But Sophie interrupted. "Something awful—"

"What happened?" asked Wil, forgetting his own news.

"Portia and Portius—" said Sophie in a stricken tone.

Wil turned to look at the stone column and was shocked to see that Portia was weeping. Tears were seeping through her stone skin and dripping in a puddle on the floor. I didn't know a stone head could cry, he thought.

"Now, Portia, beautiful you are. Please, do not cry, my dear," said Portius. "It could always be worse."

"Portius, what happened?" asked Wil.

At Wil's question, Portia wailed more.

Wil peered at her face. But nothing looked amiss.

"Portia...um...Portia...has suffered an unfortunate accident," said Portius delicately. "A skeleton ran by—"

"Was it Minister Skelch?" asked Wil. "Remember he had a skull mask?"

"We couldn't see," said Portius. "It all happened so quickly. The skeleton ran by—"

"There were two—" said Portia, sniffing.

Portius cleared his throat. "Yes, as I was saying, two skeletons ran by us and—"

"The mask of one had all but slipped off," Portia interrupted, now with profuse tears running down her cheeks.

"Yes, that's true—there were two skeletons, but almost three heads," said Portius.

"What did they do?" asked Wil.

"They...they knocked into one of Portia's braids—"

At this, Portia wailed.

"—and the tip of her braid was nicked."

"The tip of her braid?" asked Wil. "Where?"

Portia let down her braid, and Wil saw a tiny piece of the snake's snout had indeed broken off. "I can hardly see it at all, Portia."

"But you do see it, don't you? I'm blemished forever," she wailed.

Should he give Portia a handkerchief? Wil thought she might be offended—besides, she didn't exactly have any hands. He turned to Sophie, who had been listening to all this. "Shouldn't we get Mage Agassiz?" he whispered.

"I ran and got her already. She's coming," whispered Sophie back. "What happened to you?"

Still whispering, Wil told Sophie about the two skeletons in the washroom. "One said to the other, 'Don't be naive. Your position won't protect you.' Remember, Skelch had a skeleton mask? Portia and Portius wouldn't let him in until he proved he had a disguise. He must have been one of the skeletons."

"But then who was the other one?" asked Sophie.

# XXIII Gruffud's—A History

*Do you always believe what you see in a mirror?*

---

*LAPSUS LINGUAE LAPSUS CALAMI LAPSUS MEMORIAE.*
A SLIP OF THE TONGUE—LIKE A SLIP OF THE PEN—
IS A SLIP OF THE MEMORY.

---

Sophie tickled Cadmus's chin. She yawned, plumped her pillow and pulled up her covers—then cringed, just thinking about her speech for Terpsy's class that morning.

She had stood at the front of the class and cleared her throat, but her mouth felt drier than a dog biscuit.

"Gruffud's —" she had begun. Her throat had tightened. "Gruffud's was started four hundred and ninety-four years ago."

She looked down at the palm of her left hand, which was covered in ink scribbles. There were the numbers 500 and 119.

"The school will soon be 500 years old, but it has only been in MiddleGate for 119 years. Before that, Gruffud's was in Britain. But several teachers and students were killed during the Persecutions and the Burning Wall Revolt, and they burned...they burned to death."

When Sophie had practised her speech, the enormity of burning to death had escaped her. Now, she could hear desperate screams inside her head, as if she were right there by the Burning Wall.

"Charles and Espère Gruffud and three other teachers, along with their families, boarded a ship to Canada to build new lives for themselves." Sophie felt as if the words were being crushed as they crowded through the small door of her mouth.

She took another breath, but she could still hear the screams.

"They wanted to be free and they believed that snakes were powerful magical creatures. When they found out the snakes of Narcisse lived near Winnipeg, they knew this would be their new home. They never wanted to be persecuted again, and so they decided to build a secret city named MiddleGate.

"We sing Gruffud's Chant at the beginning of each school year. The words *umbris nos dedamus* mean *give ourselves to the shadows,* and Gruffud's motto is *nihil ob—obs—*

Sophie suddenly forgot what to say next. It was as if everything she had memorized scattered in splinters at her feet. She looked at her hand, but the ink scribbles had blurred to a sweaty smear. Sophie's face turned beet-red and she clutched at her sash.

"She doesn't even know Gruffud's motto," whispered Sygnithia loudly to Regina.

I've had it, thought Sophie. If Sygnithia says one more thing....

Mage Terpsy stepped to the front of the class. "Thank you, Miss Isidor," she said, in a kindly way. "Gruffud's motto is indeed *sive culex sive draco, nihil obstat. Whether mosquito or dragon, nothing stands in the way*—not even fear itself, I dare say."

Mage Terpsy had patted Sophie on the back. "There's always more to learn about Gruffud's...such an interesting, complex history."

Feeling all hot and bothered at the thought of that speech, Sophie pulled out the list of more than twenty berries they had to know for tomorrow's botanicals test and chuckled for a moment about how Peerslie had stolen Wil's list that afternoon.

She tried to study, but it was useless. That stupid Sygnithia, always teasing me, she thought. Throwing the list aside, she hopped out of bed and picked up the mirror from the bureau. One eye looked steadily back at her; the other was swallowed in the crack. She slammed the mirror down—causing Cadmus to open one sleepy, amber eye—picked up her brush and tugged savagely at her hair.

"The only person you should be mad at is...yourself. You—it's your own fault—if you'd practised more. *Nothing* stands in the way. *Nothing* stands in the way," she repeated. She looked at the palm of her hand, and there it was, right next to her thumb, *sive culex sive draco, nihil obstat*—but she'd been too nervous to see it.

Sophie sat down at her desk, pulled out a clean sheet of paper together with a pen and the bottle of ink. She looked at Cadmus's black diamond face and began to draw a skull with sunken eye sockets and a grinning mouth...then jagged, protruding teeth.

Why were two skeletons arguing in the washroom? And if Skelch were one of them, who was the other—and which one was which? What if Wil were in danger because he'd seen them?

Sophie dipped her pen and a splotch of ink dripped on the skull's left cheekbone. She turned the splotch into a tear, which trickled to the bottom of the page.

# XXIV  A Star

*What hangs beneath a crescent moon?*

---

*NUNC VIDES, NUNC NON VIDES.*
NOW YOU SEE IT, NOW YOU DON'T.

---

After moving aside a crooked pile of books from his bed, Wil crawled under the covers. With the Halloween disaster barely over and Winterlude coming soon, all the teachers were assigning more home-work than ever, in preparation for end-of-term exams. Wil pulled out the list of berries for the botanicals test. As soon as he looked at it, the memory of what happened that afternoon came flooding back.

There had been an hour to study for exams before Quartz's class. He and Sophie had gone to the library, to continue memorizing which berries were deadly poisonous and which were edible. Mage Radix's words—*Remember it's life and death if you don't know which one's which!*—rattled in Wil's head.

He had started partway down the list: rowenberry, salmonberry, shadberry, sheepberry, silverberry, snowberry, soapberry, strawberry, sugarberry, teaberry, thimbleberry, twinberry, wolfberry, young-berry...how could he possibly remember everything?

Then he had flipped back to the top of the list—blueberry, boysenberry, candleberry, checkerberry, elderberry, farkleberry, gooseberry, huckleberry, inkberry, loganberry, partridgeberry, pokeberry and raspberry.

Farkleberry—small, hard black berries. What were they used for? Something to do with diarrhea, wasn't it? Wil consulted his notes: *Extract from farkleberry root bark treats diarrhea.* "Good, got that one, at least," he murmured.

"What did you say?" asked Sophie. The frames of her eyeglasses were the colour of mouldy bread.

"Oh, nothing," said Wil. He looked over at Sophie's notes, which were filled with drawings of coloured leaves and berries.

"Those are good," said Wil. "Did you do them?"

"Yeah, it helps me study," said Sophie.

Disheartened, Wil tried writing out four columns for red, blue, yellow and white berries, when an eager voice in his ear said, "A list!"

"Oh, hi Peerslie," said Wil in a flat voice. He didn't bother looking up, because no one could see Peeping Peerslie anyhow.

"I have to learn all this for tomorrow's test."

"You are pale."

"Thanks, Peerslie, but—"

Before Wil could say another word, Peerslie snatched the paper. It flew up to the ceiling and back down several times.

"Hey, Peerslie, I need that! Give it," said Wil in a loud whisper.

Several other students looked up from their books, and Miss Heese tapped her pencil on the counter. "Shhh," she said, and she frowned at Wil.

Wil frowned at the list, which was waving in the air near the ceiling.

"Give it now, Peerslie, or I won't let you look at my homework any more," he hissed.

The piece of paper dropped very suddenly and zigzagged back down to the table.

Wil grabbed the paper, and continued running his finger along the list. "Hey, what's this? Dingleberry? I don't remember that one. *Put colour in grey hair, grow hair back if it has fallen out, tighten skin, strengthen bones, heal wounds and you won't need as much sleep.* Wil looked at Sophie questioningly. "What do dingleberries look like?"

Sophie began to giggle so much that her notes fell on the floor.

"What's the matter?" asked Wil, feeling stupid and angry all at once.

**92**

"Dingleberries are—" Sophie spluttered, but she only doubled over and began to make ugly, snorting noises.

Wil heard Peeping Peerslie sniggering somewhere high above his head near the chandelier.

"Peeping Peerslie...must...have..." Sophie managed to blurt out. She collapsed in a fit of smothered giggles.

Wil looked up towards the ceiling. The chandelier was swinging back and forth as though Peeping Peerslie too were shaking with laughter.

"Peerslie, get back down here—what's a dingleberry?" Wil whispered as loudly as he could, without having Miss Heese glare at him.

"I'm by your side, as close as a cover to a book," said Peerslie in an aggrieved tone. "No need to shout."

"I'm not—I'm not shouting," said Wil, spluttering in frustration. He glared at Peerslie— or at least where he thought Peerslie was. "What is a dingleberry anyway?"

"Well, if you must know," said Peerslie, sounding offended, "it's another word for...fartleberry!" With that, Peerslie made a rude noise and cackling, he departed.

"Peerslie, come back, you coward!" said Wil in a loud voice. He turned to Sophie. "That was really crude."

Sophie had continued to giggle long after they left the library for Mage Quartz's class. Still smarting from Peeping Peerslie's joke, Wil had tried his best as Mage Quartz urged them to cut their shadows away.

It did not go well.

"*Adumbro!*" Wil shouted, throwing all his energy into the word, willing his shadow to cut away.

It didn't budge.

"*Adumbro,*" he said half-heartedly for the fifth time. He kicked at his shadow. "Jump...run...roll over...you stupid thing. Don't just stand there!" But his shadow only sprawled on the ground sullenly—dense, grey, impermeable, immovable.

It didn't help that Sygnithia and Sylvain Sly's shadows could run in small circles, and Sophie's shadow managed one impressive jump over Quartz's head. Wil's only comfort was that Quartz had at least offered him some encouraging words.

"Right, Wychwood, I know you can do it. I've never had a student who couldn't pick up the basics of the *adumbro* charm. You'll be playing in the snapdragon championships in no time flat."

Quartz had clapped Wil so heartily on the back that Wil's shadow had quivered.

Trying to shake himself of the day, Wil drew Esme out from her hut. She coiled around his arm.

"Do you know we've been living in MiddleGate for almost half a year, Esme?"

Esme merely looked at Wil; the passage of half a year didn't seem of any great consequence to her.

As Wil stroked Esme's silken scales, he thought about the snakeskins in the cave. Perhaps the dim light in the cave had tricked their eyes—maybe there hadn't been that many snakeskins. And his suspicions about Minister Skelch did seem preposterous. Why would the Minister want to harm the very animals it was his job to protect? But those two skeletons—*Don't be naive, your position won't protect you.* One of the skeletons must have been Skelch. But who was the other one? Was it one of the teachers, or someone else?

Wil slipped the black medallion and the gold ring from around his neck. The snake on the medallion flickered under the light on the bedside table, and the ring felt oddly heavy. "I wonder what this snake symbol means. And why did Aunt Violet say *Beware the Serpent's Chain* after she had touched the medallion? And what is the Serpent's Chain?" Wil's head ached from all the questions.

Esme gazed steadily at Wil while he idly flicked the medallion's disc hanging within the crescent moon frame. The disc spun round and the tiny serpent blurred. He flicked the disc again more quickly. As the disc spun around, the golden outline of a five-pointed star flashed before his eyes for the first time—with the serpent at its centre.

"Esme, did you see that?"

Wil spun the disc again, harder, and the star glimmered for several moments.

"Look, Esme. The triangle and the arrow make a star together—a secret star."

Esme spiralled gracefully around Wil's arm; her tongue flicked several times at the medallion.

Entranced by the glimmering star, Wil spun the disc again and again, forgetting for the moment all his questions.

# XXV  The Examination

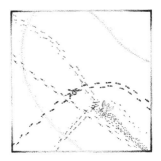

*Narrow walking paths criss-crossed Grunion Square.*

---

*IN PLUVIA AUT SOLE PROBATIO INCIPIT IN TEMPORE.*
COME RAIN, COME SHINE, AN EXAM STARTS ON TIME.

---

So much snow fell in November that Wil thought it would never stop. The first snowflakes drifted down from the sky—each one a perfect sliver of ice to catch on the tongue. The windows frosted over with crystals—glistening miniature ice mountains, fir trees and stars. The wind grew colder and whipped swirling eddies of snow high into the air. Tree branches creaked and the snow found every bit of exposed skin and pricked it without mercy. Narrow walking paths criss-crossed Grunion Square and mantles of white blanketed the Brimstone Snakes before the blizzard ended.

On a dare from Sylvain before matins one morning, Wil touched his tongue to a metal pole in Gruffud's courtyard. Horrified, he realized his tongue was stuck.

Whether out of pity or fear of punishment for egging Wil on—Wil thought the latter more likely—Sylvain ran to get Mage Radix, who came sprinting from the greenhouse with a pail filled with steaming water, which sloshed over Wil's coat. The water on his coat froze almost instantly.

"Don't you have any sense, my boy? What's that you're saying? Sylvain what? Yes, yes, that was very good of Sylvain to summon me. Don't move; you'll rip your tongue."

Wil looked sideways at Sylvain who was peering from around Mage Radix's broad back. Sylvain was staring at Wil's tongue with what appeared to be half-fascination and half-disgust, and—if there were three halves in a whole—with a half-smirk.

"Nothing a little dash of warm water won't take care of," said Mage Radix. The water released Wil's tongue easily, but it was sore for days afterwards.

Along with the shorter days, longer nights and the snow came the dreaded examinations, which were held mid-December. On the day of the numeristics exam, wooden desks in long rows lined Stone Hall. Though the carved stone creatures in the hall were not alive like Portia and Portius, Wil could imagine them coming to life and hectoring the students—especially the one just above his head. It had four horns, broad nostrils and sharp, pointed teeth, and its right hand was frozen in the act of ripping out a page from a book.

Adderson seemed to be in a fury. She strode down the aisles, inspecting everyone's palms, wrists and arms for cheat notes. She had a permanent drip hanging from the end of her nose these days, and looked disappointed at not finding any notes, until—

"What's this?" Adderson's sharp voice made Wil feel guilty, even though he'd done nothing wrong.

He swung around to see what was happening.

Adderson had picked up a small piece of paper from the floor and was holding it high in the air with a look of triumph. "Whose is this?" she said.

Chairs scraped and everybody fidgeted with their pencils. Wil heard someone snivelling. He snuck a glance at Merrily Klimchak, who was sitting behind him. Her long hair covered her face, as usual, but her shoulders were shaking. She must have been nervous about the exam. Or she had a very bad cold. Or it was her piece of paper that Adderson was clutching.

"Well, it won't do you any good now, whoever you are." Adderson pocketed the paper and continued her search for culprits.

Feeling Adderson's eyes on him, Wil hunched over in his seat. One hand clutched the medallion and ring underneath his uniform. The other hand reached into his pocket to feel Esme's smooth coils nestled there.

"We can do it, Esme," he whispered.

"There will be no talking." Stone Hall echoed with Adderson's harsh voice. "Be aware that your pencils have been treated with dehoaxing charms. Cheaters' pencils will split right down the middle."

Wil looked at the pencil on his desk with dread.

"At the sound of the bell, turn your papers over and begin. The bell will sound once at the halfway mark. At the end of the exam period, the bell will sound twice. You will stop writing and your papers will be collected." Mage Adderson paused to dab at her nose. "I wish you all—"

The sound of something dropping to the floor echoed throughout the hall.

All heads turned.

A blue egg was rolling down the aisle straight toward Mage Adderson.

But that's impossible, thought Wil. Where had it come from?

"A firebird egg!" someone shouted.

Screams filled Stone Hall; chairs scraped the floor. The sound was deafening, but abruptly all went silent.

Time was standing still, thought Wil. Sygnithia was frozen in the act of getting up from her chair. Merrily was frozen too. She was leaning down to pick up her pencil from the floor. For once, Harley was not smiling. Instead, his round face appeared to be permanently frowning.

Wil tried to move but could not. No one could move except for Adderson, who strode to the back of the hall. Why was Adderson the only one moving?

Then Wil heard someone humming. It must have been Peeping Peerslie, for the humming passed by Wil's desk and something slipped into the vacant seat in front of him. It was the first time Wil had ever seen—or rather heard—Peerslie outside the bounds of the library.

Adderson picked up the blue egg and returned to the front of the hall. She carefully placed the egg on the desk in plain sight.

"Who is responsible for *this*?" she asked in a deadly, quiet voice, at the same time as she pointed at the egg. Her eyes scanned the entire hall.

Now the silence was deafening.

Wil heard her say something that sounded like *curse-a-fairy*. Then she said, "Return to your seats at once."

Wil felt his limbs release. He quickly checked his pocket and felt for Esme. She coiled around his thumb as if to reassure him that she was perfectly fine. Once back in his seat, Wil glanced surreptitiously around the hall. No one was taking responsibility for the egg. Peerslie—it must be Peerslie, he thought. But if Peerslie had wanted to write the exam, why didn't he just sneak in quietly?

"Whoever you are...if you thought this would cancel your exam, you were sorely mistaken," said Adderson. "This egg will remain in my office for safe-keeping, until such time as the owner claims it." She picked up the black-handled brass bell. "I wish you all the very best," she said grimly, and then she rang the bell.

Stone Hall reverberated with the swishing of exam papers. Chairs scraped, and coughs answered each other from different corners of the hall. Then, only the sound of pencils scratching across paper could be heard.

Wil glanced at the exam, but couldn't resist looking again at the blue egg sitting on Adderson's table. Who would bring a firebird egg into Stone Hall, especially when it was so dangerous? If Peerslie had dropped the egg, why? What would have happened if the egg had broken? Wil could answer the last question well enough. He remembered how addled his brain became the day the firebird egg broke in the egg shop. He also remembered Mr. Egbertine saying how lucky it was the egg hadn't exploded.

Wil was distracted from thinking any more about the blue egg by the sound of Peerslie's pencil travelling speedily across the paper. Wil leaned forward to read Peerslie's exam...easy to do since Peerslie was invisible—but today, Peerslie's writing was invisible too. Not surprising—what would you expect from a ghost? Wil began to write hastily, as if everything he had studied would leak out from his brain directly onto the floor. Halfway through the exam, Wil looked up and noticed that Peerslie was gone. Fine for him—coming and going whenever he pleased.

The bell rang twice. When all the papers had been collected, everyone pushed through the doors in a great rush.

Olin Cramer was groaning. "I can't believe that question was on the exam."

"Yeah, I know," said Jinzhen. "Wouldn't you know it? Whatever I *don't* study—"

"Glad that's over," said Merrily. "So where do you think that firebird egg came from?"

"I don't know," said Sophie. "Do you really think it would kill many people?"

"And that *cursuferri* freezing charm Adderson put on us—" said Olin. "I couldn't even blink my eyes."

So Adderson froze everyone, thought Wil. That's scary, if she's able to do that.

Wil heard someone behind him whining.

"Did you get that one about how to tell if a number can be divided by 9? Did we cover that in class?"

Wil knew the answer, but only because Sophie had teased him the day before.

"The number 9 won't bite your head off. It's easy," Sophie had said. "Add up all the numerals in any number together. If you divide their sum by 9, the number itself can be divided by 9. It works for large numbers too.

"Nine is like a big basket—it holds the other numbers. One and eight, two and seven, three and six, four and five—they all add up to nine!" Sophie had said, with a look of glee.

When exam results were posted the last day of term, Wil could barely bring himself to look. Only when everyone else had left the bulletin board, did he look at the list. Sophie was on the Honour Roll. And Merrily Klimchak too. And where was his name? He reached the end of the list.

I'm not even on it! he thought.

"Mr. Wychwood, you must be pleased," said a voice, "especially since you've only come to MiddleGate so recently."

Wil whirled round to see Mage Terpsy's beaming face.

Confused, he looked back at the list and shook his head.

"You're certainly not the clop in the tass, Wychwood. But there's nothing to be ashamed of either."

"But where's my name, Mage Terpsy?"

"Where's your name, Mr. Wychwood? What are you talking about?" Mage Terpsy pointed her finger at one of the last names on the list. "You're right there, right where you should be—with the W's."

He must be going scaly if he couldn't find his own name.

*Clop in the tass*—sure. He wondered what more *tipsy-terpsies* (as everyone had taken to calling them) Mage Terpsy would come up with next. Terpsy's class had turned out to be his favourite—probably because she kept everyone on their toes with her *sword-witching*. She didn't even seem aware of the slips, and some people vied with each other to see who could collect the most in one week.

# XXVI Snapdragon

*The bird's shadow twisted into black flames.*

---

*FLAMMAM FLAMMA EXSTINGUIT.*
**FIRE FIGHTS FIRE.**

---

The icicles outside Sophie's bedroom window were longer than Sophie was tall. It was so cold that whenever they went for a walk, their eyelashes frosted over; and Aunt Violet was joking about starting a new line of cosmetics to make their fortunes—*La Neige* ice-frosted hairspray and mascara.

With school term over, everyone was busy preparing for the weeklong Winterlude festival. Houses were decorated with so many bright lights that Sophie thought they looked like giant presents. She and Wil made star ice lanterns with small candles inside to line the front walkway, and the house filled with the smells of shortbread cookies and cinnamon cakes. Aunt Violet and Aunt Rue both seemed to be covered permanently in a light dusting of flour. Even Mrs. Oleander—usually taciturn—seemed to cheer up, and had a long visit with Aunt Violet and Aunt Rue, debating the best way to make fruitcake and candied orange peel.

---

The first day of Winterlude, Aunt Violet gave Sophie and Wil a handful of blue festival coins. "Have a good time, my dears. When Rue finishes that report she's writing, we'll be visiting with the Critchleys, who've come in from out of town. We'll be in the tea tent near the ice sculptures—so you'll know where to find us."

To Sophie and Wil, it seemed as if all MiddleGate had turned out for Winterlude. Hundreds of people were drifting in and out of striped tents. Smells of hot soup and apple cider made Sophie's mouth water. By the entrance to the Winterlude grounds, giant ice sculptures glinted in the sunlight. The largest—an ice dragon—curled around an ice ruby. The creature had gnarled claws and round, bulging eyes.

"Those are scary," said Sophie, as she touched the creature's claws.

"Imagine if this thing were alive!" exclaimed Wil. "And that ruby—too bad it's not real."

"We'd be snaky rich, if it were," said Sophie, and she waved to Auguste, who was perched precariously on top of a tall, wooden ladder.

He was sculpting an immense blue ice egg higher than any tent. Below him, Mr. Egbertine hopped from one foot to another while holding the ladder; he seemed hardly able to contain himself and the ladder kept jiggling.

"*Mais...c'est, c'est...déséquilibrée*—it's lop...lopsided, Auguste," said Mr. Egbertine.

Mr. Egbertine turned suddenly to Sophie. "*Alors, Sophie, qu'est-ce que tu penses?*"

Mr. Egbertine's eyes were so wild that Sophie was lost for words. She glanced at Auguste, who shook his head.

"It's very good, Mr. Egbertine," said Sophie, even though the egg was tilting rather noticeably. Out of the corner of her eye, she saw a look of relief on Auguste's face. "If a blue egg were that big, it would probably knock out everyone in MiddleGate."

Mr. Egbertine looked so pleased that if he had had feathers, he would have been preening them, thought Sophie.

Near the ice sculptures, a man wearing a green and yellow striped robe with matching mitts was standing beside a pile of wooden rods. "Snowsnake, snowsnake!" he shouted. "Step right up and don't be shy! Break a record, you'll win a prize."

"Go on, take one, Wil," said Sophie, waiting to see the expression on Wil's face when he tried to pick up one of the rods.

Wil chose a long red and black rod.

The rod immediately turned into a writhing, red and black snake, and Sophie burst out laughing at Wil's look of horror.

"What am I supposed to do with it?" he asked.

"Just throw it," she answered.

"But it's wriggling too much." He dropped the snake, and it promptly turned back into a rod.

"Just hold it by the tail," said Sophie. "The one that slides the furthest wins."

Sophie picked up a pure white snowsnake with gleaming black eyes. She threw it and it skittered until coming to rest near the end of the snow mound.

Wil tried again, but the next rod turned into a limp black snake, even when he grasped it by the tail. He threw the snake down in apparent frustration, and it turned back into a wooden rod. "I'm hungry," he said, sounding annoyed. "Let's get something to eat."

They headed over to the towering Ice Palace to buy hollow chunks of ice that were filled to the brim with hot chocolate—you had to drink it quickly before the ice melted—and to munch on steaming chunks of meat skewered on wooden spears. Then Sophie tried one of the triple icicles with nine layers—each one had a different fruit flavour— and Wil exchanged one of his blue coins for fluffy snow candy, which floated off in the wind if you weren't careful.

They stopped to watch the younger children, who were playing string games with a glowing blue rope. The children wove in and out of each other's paths to make patterns against the snow—there was the bouncing snowman, the snake's tail, the burning bush and the rabbit in the moon.

In the middle of the Winterlude grounds sprawled an enormous hill of snow and ice. Dozens of people were standing on top of it and clapping their hands.

"What's going on there?" asked Wil.

"Wait until you see," said Sophie with a big grin.

They clambered up a set of uneven steps gouged into the side of the hill. Slipping and sliding, and breathless by the time they reached the top of the hill, Sophie watched Wil's expression turn to one of astonishment as he looked at the long ditch carved right through the middle of the mound.

"It's deep, isn't it?" she said. "It's for ditchball."

"This is where we're going to be playing?" asked Wil, craning his neck to see the other end of the deep ditch.

At that moment, two players strode into the ditch and everyone around them clapped and cheered.

"What are they doing?" asked Wil.

"It's a snapdragon duel," Sophie replied, hardly able to contain herself with excitement. "Let's get closer so we can see."

At the gong of the bell, the first player's shadow twisted into the shape of a monstrous dragon with ragged, flapping wings.

"They usually start out with a dragon," said Sophie. "That's why it's called snapdragon."

The second player hesitated a moment and changed his shadow into a small mouse, which ran up the shadow of the dragon's long tail.

The shadow of the dragon's tail lashed to and fro, trying to dislodge the shadow of the mouse. The dragon's jaws snapped at the small creature's shadow, but the mouse shadow ran up to the top of the dragon's head, where it perched and began to groom its whiskers. The crowd laughed and clapped.

The dragon's shadow reared up on its hind legs. Leaping into the air, the dragon shadow turned into a cat shadow, and the cat shadow lunged at the mouse shadow.

Quick as a wink, the mouse shadow turned into a monstrous bird's shadow, and swooped down on the cat's shadow.

The cat's shadow turned just as quickly into the shadow of a jagged rock.

The bird's shadow clenched its talons, twisted into black flames and engulfed the rock.

The shadow of the rock turned to black fire.

"Black fire fights black fire," said Sophie. "I've never seen the shadows do that before."

But the day clouded over suddenly and the shadows lost their strength. Just as the players called a truce, Sophie glanced over at Will—whose expression was one of not-a-chance-I'll-ever-be-able-to-do-that—and burst out laughing.

———

That night, the Ice Palace sparkled like a brilliant jewel. The fireworks ended at midnight with a winged dragon—it must have had a hundred heads. The dragon spiralled high above the festival grounds and burst into flaming sparks and puffs of smoke with a dying scream. Wil dreamt all night about flaming dragons, black shadows and the ditch—that deep ditch.

# XXVII The Snow King's Secret

*What can you see deep inside a blue jewel?*

---

*NOLI VIVUM CONTEMNERE*

*ETIAMSI NULLAS PALPEBRAS*

*NULLAS AURES*

*NULLA MEMBRA HABEAT.*

DESPISE NOT ANY LIVING CREATURE

EVEN SHOULD IT POSSESS NO EYELIDS

NO EARS NOR LEGS.

---

B lue jewels shimmered against the glistening walls inside the Ice Palace. Minister Skelch shivered, inspected his reflection in the mirror and then squirmed on the wooden bench.

Those double chins—where had they come from? he thought. I ought to lose a bit of...but don't I look like the spitting image of my father? Just squint, and it's as if my own father were sitting right there. Fine for a man of my stature to carry a bit extra—conveys a sense of solidity. A man people can trust, you know.

Minister Skelch squirmed again. It was taking far too long to glue the wretched things on...

Dolores Hinkle, her hair white as snow, put her brush down on a table filled with sparkling blue jewels. Lips pursed, she stood back to examine her handiwork. The blue jewels shimmered against the glistening walls of the Ice Palace.

"Just a few more jewels, Your Honour. You must sit still, sir." She glued another small, round jewel to Minister Skelch's cheek. "You make one of the finest Snow Kings I've ever seen. Remember the day your father—"

Why did I agree to be Snow King in the first place? thought Minister Skelch. An honour to be asked anyhow, and wasn't it my dream when I watched my own father drop the ditchball into the ditch? Delores Hinkle had been a young woman then, hair black as crow's wings; she had always been a chatterbox.

I remember my very first game of ditchball—I couldn't have been more than ten years old—knocked down in the first five minutes. What was the name of that tricky fellow with the red hair? Rupert, Ruford, Rudolph, Ru...Ru...Rufus—yes, that was it. Rufus rammed into him, and the referee didn't even call the penalty. I, Erro Skelch, was carried out of the ditch and missed the whole game.

"But we won." Minister Skelch chuckled.

"What's that, Your Honour?"

"Oh, nothing at all, Dolores. Fine job you're doing."

"Why, thank you, sir. May my poor mother, rest her soul, be proud. When I was young, she always let me put one gem on."

Minister Skelch grimaced. Wretched things—tougher than snake scales—I'd like to pull every last one of them off, he thought.

"—remember your father like it was yesterday." Dolores Hinkle carefully applied another blue crystal to the very tip of Minister Skelch's nose.

The sun had already set, but ditchball could not begin without the Snow King. Minister Skelch took a deep breath; it would all be over soon.

By Draco, I should enjoy myself, he thought. Now that winter's here, those miserable snakes at Narcisse are wintering out of sight. Grotesque creatures—no eyelids, no ears, no legs—and always creeping low to the ground. A man of my position and responsibilities can't let on that he loathes snakes. I would be politically penniless...ruined!

Minister Skelch looked down at his knee-high blue fakesnake boots. He shuddered and forced himself to smile. "Dolores, excellent job, just like your mother before you. My compliments."

**105**

With a deep breath, Minister Skelch dismissed all thoughts of snakes from his mind, and drew himself to his full height, crown and all. The next moment, he strode out from the Ice Palace, his cloak sweeping across the snow. Blue jewels flashed by the light of the torches as he waved gravely to the crowds, who cheered at his appearance. Never had there been such a regal Snow King.

# XXVIII  Battle in the Ditch

*Look to the north. Will you find the stars of Draco?*

---

*PILAM SPECTA.*

**KEEP YOUR EYE ON THE BALL.**

---

A sprawling orange and white striped tent had been set up near the ditchball hill. Inside smelled of soggy wool mittens, rubber boots and mothballs. The grade fives were getting ready for their first game of ditchball. Wil eyed his pile of gear and thick padding, which Aunt Rue had hauled out of the attic for him.

The annual ditchball games started after sunset on the last day of the Winterlude Carnival. Teams of seven from each grade vied against each other, with girls against girls and boys against boys—Nox wearing black and silver versus Lux, blue and gold.

Wil shivered at the thought of the ditchball—a large rainbow-coloured ball as tall as he was. They had been practicing in Thistleburn Field with Mage Quartz for the past month. As far as Wil could tell, ditchball was like a tug-of-war, only with a ball instead of a rope.

"Right," Mage Quartz had said at their first practice. "Make sure you keep your eye on the ditchball at all times—it's got a mind of its own sometimes." He had grinned at the class as he said this.

"The night of the game, the ditchball is dropped by the Snow King down into the middle of the great ditch. Object of the game—score a goal by lifting the ditchball to your goalie platform at ditch's end. A goal is worth three points. All's fair except you may not hit, kick, tackle, gang up on, or otherwise injure another player. Penalty for kitting, kicking, tackling, ganging up on, or otherwise injuring another player—you're out at least one whole minute."

Wil hurried to pull on his thick leg pads. Harley Weeks and Olin Cramer, already dressed in their black and silver jerseys, were parading around in front of the Lux team. Wil eased into the shoulder and chest pads, tightened the leather belt around his waist and slipped on Nox's black and silver jersey.

"Hurry up, Wychwood, or you'll miss the game," said Sylvain Sly, who was wearing Lux's blue and gold jersey. He was strutting back and forth, flexing his padded arms to Lux cheers and Nox jeers. Suddenly he started chanting:

> *Ditch, ditch! Bewitch the ditch!*
> *A stitch, a snitch, a switch, the ditch!*
> *A quitch, a scritch, the ditch, the ditch!*

Sylvain was soon joined by the others. The tent walls seemed to balloon with the hullabaloo, until Quartz popped his head into the tent.

"Best save your energies for the game, laddies."

Trying to ignore Sylvain, who was still parading back and forth, Wil tied up his boots and pulled on his helmet.

"All right, let's have a go then!" shouted Quartz. He opened the flap of the tent and waved them out. "Ready or not...to the *ditch!*"

They stepped out into the clear, cold night air, following Quartz past the snowcone stand. The snow squeaked with every footstep, and each breath froze in a frosty cloud. Shivering with the cold—or maybe he was just nervous—Wil looked at all the people standing on top of the gargantuan hill. It seemed much higher than when he'd seen it last. In the torchlight, looming shadows flickered on the ice walls of the ditch. Lee Hopebone, Nox's goalie, was already perched high above Wil's head on the wooden platform that stretched from one side of the ditch to the other. The great ditch curved around to the Lux goalie at the other end.

"Everybody to their places!" shouted Quartz, who was standing at the top of the ditch in the middle.

The crowd at the top of the ditch began to chant, *Ditch, ditch! Bewitch the ditch!*

But when the Snow King stepped forward beside Mage Quartz, the crowd fell silent.

Wil's stomach churned as he stared up at the Snow King—it was Minister Skelch. Although the identity of the Snow King was supposed to be secret, everybody knew it anyway. But even if Skelch were a murderer, he looked every inch the part of the Snow King, from his swirling cloak to his tall crown of blue jewels.

The Snow King took the ditchball from the two men who were holding it. The ditchball trembled and pulled forward, as if willing itself to be dropped. Quartz blew his piercing silver whistle three times. Amidst the roar of the crowd, the giant ditchball dropped straight down and landed with a thud.

Wil ran forward at full tilt and pushed against the ditchball with all his might. The ditchball wavered, and Nox inched it forward.

Sylvain Sly toppled over him. "Get lost, Woodwhich."

Wil jumped on top of Sylvain. "No way!" Anything to keep Sylvain from getting the ditchball.

Quartz's silver whistle pierced the air again. "One minute for Wychwood!"

Wil paced back and forth in the wooden penalty pen at the end of the ditch. After what seemed like an hour instead of a minute, Quartz gave a short, sharp whistle, and waved in Wil's direction. Wil dashed out into the ditch. Nox had managed to push the ditchball all the way to the end of the ditch. Slipping and sliding along the ice, Wil scrambled to help lift the ditchball to Lee Hopebone, but Sylvain began pulling at Wil's legs.

Stretched out full length on the platform, Lee held out his arms as far as he could. "Come on—I've got it...I've got it...I've...got...it—"

But the ditchball slipped from Lee's grasp and Jinzhen pulled it away. "Close, Nox, close. Keep it up! You'll have another chance," someone in the crowd yelled.

Lux carried the ditchball away, and Wil thought for a moment the ditchball was a giant insect on legs. Harley and Olin managed to yank the ball from Lux, and twirled it around. The ditchball skittered along the walls of the ditch towards Wil, who had hung back near Lee. Wil slid towards the goalie's platform with the ditchball and somehow lifted it up to Lee all by himself.

Two whistle blasts. "Three points to Nox," shouted Quartz.

"Go Nox! Go Nox!" shouted the onlookers, waving small black and silver flags wildly in the air.

Harley slapped Wil on the back. "Good job, Wil!"

Quartz blew his whistle twice. "Nox and Lux to the middle!"

The Nox team threw the ditchball up to the top of the ditch. The Snow King caught it and held it high above his head. The torches flared, and the jewels on the Snow King's face glistened.

The ditchball dropped.

In a surprise move, two Lux players, who were taller than Wil, caught the ditchball before it even hit the ground. They threw it over to Sylvain, who carried it off. The Lux blues howled past to their goalie.

Blue flags waved madly, and the crowd roared, "Lux—Lux—LUX!"

Two whistle blasts. "Lux scores!" shouted Quartz.

Wil walked back to the middle, still fuming at Sylvain.

*Ditch, ditch, bewitch the ditch!* the crowd chanted.

Distracted, Wil forgot to watch for the ditchball. It dropped down right on top of him, and he was thrown against the icy side of the ditch. A jolt of pain shot through his right shoulder, and he fell senseless to the ground.

---

Lanterns hung from ropes, casting eerie shadows on the tent walls of the makeshift infirmary. Master Meninx was busy tending to a man with a swollen nose. The man's companion boasted a shining purple welt over his left eye.

Drifting in and out of a daze, Wil heard a woman's voice comforting a sobbing child. "Here's a hug, dear. There, there, you're safe now."

"Rough game," said someone in a gruff voice.

When next he woke, Wil saw two whitish balls wavering in front of him.

"Are you all right, Wil?" asked a voice that sounded familiar. "It was nine to three! Nox won. Wil, can you hear me?"

Now one ball was floating in front of Wil's eyes. No, it's a head, he thought, but where's the rest of its body? He tried to raise himself from the pillow. "One," he said.

But there were hundreds of chanting voices in his head.

"SSSerpent's Chain...SSSerpent's Chain...SSSnow King...SSSerpent's Chain," he mumbled, his words slurring.

"Serpent's Chain? The Snow King? Wil, what are you talking about?" asked the voice.

"Ssssss..." Wil sank back down onto his pillow with a long sigh.

———⌒∿⌒———

"Wil, Wil. Can you hear me?" asked Sophie. "What about the Serpent's Chain?"

Wil's eyes were sunken and closed. Sophie drew a sharp breath. The snake on Wil's black medallion was glowing. Looking around furtively at the shadows on the tent wall, Sophie pulled the covers up over Wil to hide the medallion.

Master Meninx bustled into the tent. "Time for you to go now, Miss Isidor. Don't you worry. Mr. Wychwood will be sound as a snake. He's just groggy and needs to rest. Time for you to go now."

"But I need to stay with him, so he'll be safe, Master Meninx, he keeps talking about the Serpent's Chain ..." Sophie's voice trailed off at Master Meninx's stern look. Before Sophie could say anything more, Meninx hustled her from the tent.

———⌒∿⌒———

Master Meninx watched the northern lights pulsing across the sky. They seemed so close—as if they were calling him, as if he could almost touch them. Then he shook himself of the cold, and bustled back into the tent.

"Young man, you've certainly —"

He stopped short.

The bed was empty.

———⌒∿⌒———

Above the festival grounds, the northern lights twisted across the sky beneath Draco's constellation—like a great shimmering serpent of blues and greens. Earthbound laughter and merrymaking tickled its underbelly.

The shimmering serpent lights disappeared...then glimmered again.

# XXIX Firecatchers

*Missing...*

---

### O, LOCUS DELICTI.
### O, THE SCENE OF THE CRIME.

The two Firecatchers filled the tent with their long, crimson cloaks. One skirted around Wil's bed, then swept from the tent to scour outside.

"I...I don't understand," stuttered Master Meninx. "He was alone...but only for a moment."

"You're sure he didn't leave by himself?" said the second Firecatcher, whose voice was unmistakably female.

Master Meninx shook his head.

"Not under his own steam," said Master Meninx. His shadow on the tent wall trembled from the flickering light of the lantern, and seemed overshadowed by the Firecatcher's shadow. "I was looking at the night sky," said Master Meninx. "The Northern Lights were...so dramatic—"

The Firecatcher leaned closer; the acrid smoke that clung to her cloak swirled around Master Meninx.

"Master Meninx, think," said the Firecatcher. "Who was here tonight?"

"A man with a bloody nose," said Master Meninx, "and one with a swollen eye. They bragged about what fine Snow Kings they'd make. Then Mage Quartz brought Mr. Wychwood in."

"Who else?" asked the Firecatcher.

Master Meninx's brow furrowed. "A lost child, but her mother picked her up."

"No one else?"

"I'm, I'm not sure." Master Meninx began to feel flustered from all the questions.

"Master Meninx, you must be able to tell us something."

Meninx mustered some of his bristling demeanour. "But I'm telling you everything I know."

The second Firecatcher returned to the tent. Master Meninx was now standing between the two Firecatchers; the pungent smoke eddied around his head.

"William Wychwood was lying in bed," said the first Firecatcher in a deep voice. "You stepped outside; when you returned...he was gone."

"Yes, that's right," said Master Meninx, his voice cracking. "Just the Snow King—

"The Snow King?"

"Yes, the Snow King checked in on the lad briefly, then returned to ditchball."

The two Firecatchers turned and though they said nothing, they seemed to be conferring with one other.

"And Mr. Wychwood's cousin came too—Miss Isidor," blurted Master Meninx. "She wanted to stay, but he needed rest." He stared at the wall of the tent; the shadow of the lantern chain was swaying back and forth hypnotically. "Maybe it's better...it's better she left," he muttered.

"Why?" said one of the Firecatchers, her voice sharp.

"She said—" said Master Meninx. "She mumbled something about the Serpent's Chain," said Master Meninx.

The two Firecatchers stiffened.

"It was just nonsense, though," said Master Meninx. "Children do go on sometimes."

———

Outside, crowds were still chanting *Ditch, ditch! Bewitch the ditch!* Ice dancers wearing tall icicle crowns skated hand-in-hand in a long sinuous line on the frozen river. The fire dancers by the Ice Palace twirled balls of fire so quickly the lines of fire looked like spiral snakes, and the torch flames on top of the Ice Palace shot high into the sky, rivalling the northern lights dancing above.

**113**

# XXX  Prisoner

*A key turned in the lock.*

---

*RES IN CARDINE EST.*

**THINGS LOOK SERIOUS.**

Snow crunched under steady footsteps. The grip around Wil's ribs tightened; he could hardly breathe and his eyes and mouth were bound tightly with a cloth. He was being carted roughly on someone's back—like a sack of potatoes.

The chain...is the chain still around my neck? he thought in a sudden panic.

He pulled his left hand free and fumbled for the medallion and the ring. He could feel them both, warm and reassuring. He yanked the chain clasp and the medallion and ring fell into his hand.

The footsteps slowed, a door opened and a gush of stale air fanned Wil's face. His head bumped against something hard, and he heard the sound of cloth ripping. Keys rattled...and another door opened. Without warning, he was flung unceremoniously down on the floor.

His captor's footsteps receded, and Wil was left alone.

Wil pulled his other hand free and managed to loosen the blindfold around his eyes. By the light of the tiny serpent on the medallion, he seemed to be in a large, dark storage room filled with wooden crates. His head and right shoulder both throbbing, he scanned the floor and found a hollow crack large enough to hide the ring and medallion. He pushed one of the crates over the hole—and not a moment too soon.

Footsteps returned.

Wil quickly slumped over, his eyes closed.

A chair scraped across the floor, and Wil was hoisted onto it. His hands were bound again and his blindfold tightened. He couldn't see anything, but at least the binding around his mouth was removed.

"Water—" he croaked.

"Of course, some water," said a man's voice. "You've been a good keeper."

Wil slurped greedily at a cup of water held to his lips.

"We have looked long and hard for it," said the voice.

"Who—who are you? What's a k-k-keeper?" Wil could hardly speak, his head was hurting so.

"If you're wise, you'll give it to us—now."

"Give what?"

"No games, boy," said the voice, now harsh. "The black medallion—where's the black medallion?"

"I—I don't know what you're talking about," Wil repeated, his voice trembling.

"You're lying, boy." Rough hands ripped Wil's shirt open. "By Draco, what have you done with it?"

The rough hands searched Wil's pockets, but found nothing. The man cursed again, the door clanged shut and a key turned in the lock, leaving Wil in darkness.

# XXXI The Curse

*Why can't time stand still?*

---

*TEMPUS NEMINEM MANET.*

TIME STANDS STILL FOR NO ONE.

---

The grandfather clock chimed four o'clock. Unable to sleep, Sophie crept down the stairs and peered through the kitchen door keyhole. Aunt Rue and Aunt Violet were sitting at the table by the light of a spluttering candle.

Aunt Violet eyed the dregs of the tea leaves in her cup. "It's no use, Rue." Aunt Violet's hands trembled as she put the cup down. "The tea leaves are caked together."

For the first time Sophie thought, Aunt Violet is getting old.

"If I hadn't come home early..." said Aunt Rue, "but Minister Skelch wanted that report on the bees finished."

"Rue, it's not your fault," said Aunt Violet. "Don't blame yourself. The Firecatchers will find him."

"But he was hurt. We should have been there." Aunt Rue twisted her hands together. "They've forgotten my brother Cyril, haven't they?" she asked in a choked voice.

Aunt Rue and Aunt Violet both stared at the candle flame, as if willing it to relinquish news of Wil's whereabouts.

The candle crackled, then fizzled as the wick drowned in wax. Only a sliver of waning moonlight glimmered through the windowpane.

"Do you remember you sang that song about the Serpent's Chain?" asked Aunt Rue.

Aunt Violet stood up; her chair scraped the floor.

"Sshhh, you'll wake up Sophie," whispered Aunt Rue.

"I...I...don't recall," said Aunt Violet, her voice quavering.

"That black medallion he has—" said Aunt Rue, without finishing her sentence. A tear rolled down her cheek. "And I keep thinking about my sister Ivy...about the last time I saw her. My mother was beside herself—do you remember?"

Aunt Violet nodded silently.

"She said, 'For serpent's sake, Ivy, that Wychwood woman hates magic. If you marry her son Virgil...you're on your own. Leave us and go to your destiny.' *Leave us...Leave us...Leave us...*That curse echoes in my mind."

"That was the last time we saw her," said Aunt Violet in a dull voice. "And we didn't even know that Ivy and Virgil had a child."

Sophie couldn't bear to listen any more, and crept back up the stairs. She fell into a fitful sleep broken by a nightmare. She had fallen into a wooden box painted coal-black. It turned into a soft, spongy, suffocating black mass, like a pillow that had no edges.

# XXXII  A Clue

*Don't be distracted by the heads, for the claws be sharp.*

---

*REDI AD LOCUM FACINORIS.*

**RETURN TO THE SCENE OF THE CRIME.**

---

I t was two days since Wil had gone missing. Term had already begun, and classes were running much as usual. Sophie sat down in Mage Tibor's class—by far her favourite class, because they got to draw maps and colour them.

Mage Tibor was convinced there was more than one gate leading beyond the bounds of MiddleGate, and had been scouring MiddleGate's historical records. "The house with the five-pointed stars is undoubtedly the largest gateway," he said. "But there must have been others— forgotten, perhaps, or even secret."

Everyone else had already pulled out their maps of MiddleGate and started to work on them. As she unrolled her map, Sophie heard Sygnithia Sly whispering, "...serves him right. That family has had it coming for years."

Sophie's cheeks flushed and she knocked over her bottle of green ink; it splattered over her map, turning Grunion Square and the Brimstone Snakes a nasty green.

Mage Tibor hurried over. "My dear...hmmm...how dreadful! A splotch on your beautiful map."

In horror, Sophie watched as the stain slowly spread.

"There, there, my dear." Mage Tibor patted her shoulder. "I've got some special...hmmm... vanishing compound that will do the trick."

———cʌɔ———

In numeristics, Adderson decided to give a surprise quiz—as she put it, "to see how much you've forgotten over the holidays."

At the end of class, Sophie handed in a completely blank quiz.

Mage Adderson, who rarely showed signs of sympathy for anyone, handed the test back to Sophie. "Er—" Mage Adderson paused and cleared her throat. "—perhaps you could tackle these questions another time, Miss Isidor. You and Mr. Wychwood can work on them together if—I mean, when he is found."

Sophie hadn't the stomach for lunch. Instead, she collected her jacket and mitts from her locker and walked along the corridor towards Portia and Portius. They were both fast asleep. Disappointed, Sophie took off her eyeglasses to see what colour they were.

Grey—exactly how she felt.

A voice—an unpleasant, nasal voice—interrupted her thoughts.

"... mewling and puling over Wychwood."

Sophie put her eyeglasses back on, in time to see Sygnithia Sly peering from around the other side of the column, with an ugly grin on her face.

Then Sophie heard Regina Piehard sniggering from behind the column. "That family specializes in disappearing acts, doesn't it?"

"It's sickening how much he likes to draw attention to himself, isn't it?" said Sygnithia, still smirking at Sophie from behind the column. "Poor Willy Winkums. I say, good riddance!"

"Why don't you go get lost yourselves!" Sophie yelled, and she stepped around to the other side of column.

"Oh, look who's defending Willy? Miss Dizzy herself," said Sygnithia.

"Miss Sly and Miss Piehard, such bullying is not tolerated at Gruffud's," said Portia, whose eyes were now wide open. Portia's voice was so cold and angry that Sophie was sure she would have stamped her foot, if she had had one.

Sygnithia only giggled and ran off with Regina.

"One must rise above such insults," said Portia, who looked at Sophie with pity, then turned to Portius. "Class bully—there's one every year, isn't there, Portius?"

**119**

Portius opened one eye and nodded his head sleepily. "At least one every year, and sometimes two or three."

"Mr. Wychwood is undoubtedly most worthy of our worry," said Portia, her voice now sounding impatient. "That he is missing is a sorry trial, but surely—" Portia paused while Portius yawned. Then they intoned together:

> *If we were you*
> *But we are not*
> *To the crime scene*
> *We would hop.*

Sophie hugged the column. "Portia, Portius, of course," she said. "What a good idea!" Then she hurried off, calling behind her, "Thank you, Portia, thank you Portius, you always know what to do. Have a good nap."

"We wish you well, Sophie Isidor," said Portius, gazing after Sophie. "She carries a great burden, Portia, doesn't she?"

Portia nodded and smiled sadly.

Portius shook himself of his sleepiness and said briskly, as if to vanquish Portia's sadness. "My compliments, Portia dear. Just think if we were the hydra and had seven heads—what you and I could do!" Portius broke into a fervent song and serenaded his lovely Portia.

> *What time we have*
> *On this earthly plain*
> *Is given over to mortal pain,*
> *Seize the moment and seize the day,*
> *For even the mighty Ozymandias*
> *Was slain.*

Both heads chortled and yawned together. Then they settled in again for their afternoon nap, but not before cajoling one of the braided serpents into keeping a lookout.

———◌◌◌———

The festival grounds were derelict, the Ice Palace broken and crumbling. The hill and ditch were flattened; nothing but misshapen boulders and splinters of the wooden platforms remained. Scattered across the snow were melted candles, lost mittens, trailing scarves, half-eaten pieces of snakecake and candied marzipan, ragged bits of string and bootlaces and a snowsnake snapped in half.

Sophie picked up the two pieces of the snowsnake.

"Nothin' much you can do with those, little lady," said a deep voice. "Once a snowsnake's broke, no spirit left. Bes' jus' burn 'em."

Sophie turned around and met the blue, rheumy eyes of a stooped man with a shovel in his hand. She dropped the pieces of the snowsnake as if she'd been caught stealing something, and they clattered together on the ground. The man bent over with a grunt, picked them up and tossed them onto a large woodpile.

"Wha' you doin' 'ere anywho, all alone?" he asked. "Shouldn't you be at school? Not safe for youngsters to be out by theirselves—not when there's such foul things goin' on. You should go home—skedaddle now."

"I...I...I lost my...my mother's watch during Winterlude," said Sophie. "It dropped, it was right around here, I think. My mother was so upset."

"And you're only looking now?" The man eyed her with suspicion and shook his head mournfully. "Didn't you 'ear about that boy disappeared the other day? What can the world be coming to? Be a long winter—bad omen, if you ask me." He shook his head again, and continued to pick up stray bits and pieces of debris.

"I won't be long. I'm checking, in case..." said Sophie. "Thank you," she added in a singsong voice, which she hoped sounded casual.

The man only grunted and then wandered off, still grumbling about bad omens.

Sophie scoured the ground for the four hollows in the snow where the legs of Wil's cot had been. She found them, bent down and scraped away some of the trampled snow around the hollows.

Nothing.

But then she caught sight of small, shiny stones.

Seven small jewels hidden in the snow.

Sophie picked one up and held it against the sun—it was a tiny, perfect, chilling sapphire jewel.

"The Snow King," whispered Sophie to herself. "Minister Skelch."

She gathered up the remaining jewels, stuffed them into her pocket and started walking away as quickly as she could from the grounds. The old man was digging on the other side of the field near the remains of the Ice Palace. As she reached the woodpile, Sophie smiled broadly and pulled the two pieces of snowsnake out from underneath a broken chair.

# XXXIII  An Eye

*Have you ever felt as if someone (or something) were watching you?*

---

*NIHIL EXIGUUM EST, QUIA PARVA SIGNIFICANT MAGNA.*

**NOTHING IS INSIGNIFICANT,**

**FOR THE SMALL POINTS TO THE LARGE.**

---

Sophie climbed the steps of the Secretariat on the Status of Magical Creatures building, which was one of her favourites—covered in terra cotta peacocks, fishes, salamanders, beavers, eagles and snakes, alongside vines and sheaves of wheat.

Standing on tiptoe and peering through the windows of the dark oak door, Sophie saw two guards at the front desk. What if they didn't let her in? There was a young man whom she didn't know. The other man put down his newspaper. With relief, she saw it was Olly Tipperwall, who always gave her licorice.

Seeing someone at the door, Olly Tipperwall stretched, got up from his chair and sauntered over to the door. He looked through the window; his face broke out into a wide grin and the door swung open noiselessly.

"That you, little Sophie? You was scarcely up to my kneecap. Now look at you! Your aunt's still up in her office, working a little later than usual. You go on up, there's a good girl."

Sophie smiled at him and looked surreptitiously above his head at the directory for the building. She scanned the list quickly. The Minister of the Secretariat was on the top floor.

The young man was eyeing Sophie with apparent suspicion. "Do you have identification?" he asked, his voice stiff.

"Come on, Stan," interrupted Olly Tipperwall. "No need to be so officious. This is Rue Isidor's little niece—Rue Isidor in the Dangerous Insects Division."

Sophie knew it was Endangered Insects, but decided not to say anything.

Olly Tipperwall rummaged in his pockets. "Piece of licorice?"

———

Sophie had never been on the top floor. Luckily, the corridor was empty; everyone must have left for the day. Chewing nervously on a stringy piece of black licorice, she tiptoed down a long, silent hallway of highly polished black and white tiles. Oak doors lined the hallway, each with gold leaf letters on pebbled glass.

Sophie looked to her left.

*Mme. Lucretia Daggar,*
*Senior Assistant to the Deputy Minister*

That means the Deputy Minister would be next, and the Deputy Minister would be near the Minister, thought Sophie, or was it the other way around? She tried to remember what the word *deputy* meant and walked past several doors, without even reading the names on them.

Then she noticed a door at the end of the hallway, which had large gold letters on it. Even from a distance, the letters were easy to read:

*E. Sibelius Skelch*
*Minister*
*Secretariat on the Status*
*of*
*Magical Creatures*

Sophie walked quickly to the end of the hallway and leaned against the door. No sound. She turned the brass doorknob slowly. Her heart jumped as the door squeaked open.

The walls of the Minister's office were filled with paintings of monstrous creatures—feathered, furry, hairy, scaly, horned and winged. The largest painting—it filled the whole wall behind the Minister's desk—was of a gruesome creature with the head of a lion, the body of a goat and a long tail. It was clutching a struggling peacock in its claws and vomiting flames.

The peacock didn't stand a chance.

Sophie felt sick and looked away, but her eyes fell on a glass jar sitting on the Minister's desk. The jar filled with gelatinous, swampy-green liquid—and something else.

She crept closer. What was that thing?

She gagged.

It was a large, bloated eye. And it seemed to be looking right at her, even when she moved.

Doing her best to ignore both the painting of the lion-goat and the eye in the jar, she riffled through the papers on the desk. There were letters thanking the Minister for coming to speak to the Herpetological Society, and a letter inviting him to next summer's Dragonfly Festival at Birds Hill—nothing unusual.

She poked under the desk and found a wooden box. Inside was a cloak with blue jewels.

"The Snow King's cloak," she whispered.

She dragged the cloak from under the desk and swirled it around her shoulders—but wait... there was a long rip, and a piece of the cloak was missing. Sophie fingered the ragged threads.

Then her eyes caught sight of a pile of blue jewels on the desk.

She stuffed the cloak back in the box and picked up a jewel from the desk. Holding it up to the light, she brought out one of the jewels she had found in the snow from her pocket.

Both...cold, sapphire blue.

"These jewels must be from the cloak," she muttered. "Maybe Wil was fighting back and ripped the cloak."

Sophie scooped up a handful of the blue jewels and then tried to open one of the desk drawers. Locked. All the drawers were locked.

As she looked around, she saw a small scrap of paper on the floor. It was a doodle of a snake—more like a slug—and not a very good doodle, at that.

"Why, what a surprise, Miss Isidor!"

Sophie froze and the piece of paper fluttered to the floor.

Minister Skelch seemed to have appeared from practically nowhere. She hadn't even heard the door open.

"Are you looking for your aunt's office?" asked the Minister. Without waiting for Sophie to answer, he added, "It's down on the eight floor, just to the left of the stairs. Er, bad news about your cousin. I'm so sorry...ahem...hmmm...terrible situation. He'll be found soon, I'm sure." The Minister looked at Sophie apologetically. "And is there something I can help you with?"

Without thinking, Sophie said the first thing that came into her head. "I was coming up the stairs...and I thought...I heard a scream coming from this office...and um, I opened the door, but no one was here. It must have been somewhere, someone else, the scream, I mean...and I like your paintings—" Sophie babbled and ended lamely. She pointed at the eye, which was staring intently at them both. "Is that a real eye?"

The Minister's eyes twinkled behind his eyeglasses. "My predecessor, Archibald Scrimmer, was quite a collector, as you can see. But a scream, you say?"

Sophie squirmed. The Minister's smile deepened; his double chins became triple chins. "Well, I'll alert Mr. Tipperwall at the front desk. And yes, there's a story about that eye. But we don't want to give a little girl any nightmares, do we?

I am not a *little girl*, thought Sophie, but she held her tongue.

Minister Skelch smiled broadly. "Those eyeglasses of yours are quite something, aren't they," he said. "Just changed colour from mauve to a nice tiger-stripe pattern."

# XXXIV Footsteps

*There must be a way out.*

---

*NE CEDE MALIS.*

**DO NOT GIVE UP.**

---

Wil had managed to loosen his bindings. His shoulder aching and stomach growling, he edged his way along the floor in pitch black darkness. His lips were dry and cracked. He longed for one of Mr. Bertram's mints and a drink of cool water. He thought wistfully of Esme, and hoped that Sophie was taking care of her.

Amidst some small pebbles on the floor, his fingers finally found what he was looking for—a wavering crack. He followed the crack to its end. This must be the right one, he thought. There was the crate on top of it. He pushed at the crate with his shoulder and scoured the floor for the hollow. There, still nestled safely—the ring and the medallion. The thick darkness of the room seemed to be trying to swallow up the tiny glowing serpent on the medallion.

Footsteps approached...

He froze and held his breath. Should he shout for help—but what if it was that man again?

The footsteps passed the door.

Silence.

Wil heard a faint sound—like a chair scraping along a floor—above his head. A fine mist of dust fell on his head, and he sneezed. He stuffed the ring inside one of his pockets, and as an afterthought, picked up some of the pebbles from the floor. Then he held the medallion up high above his head, casting a small circlet of light onto the ceiling.

Footsteps approached again, and keys jingled in the lock...but the door remained shut.

"Serpent's blood," said a man's voice.

Wil waited, holding his breath, his heart pounding.

The keys jingled again and the footsteps receded away.

# XXXV Found

*Why salamanders and spiders, but no serpents and snakes?*

---

*QUAM SCANDALOSUM LIBRUM PERDERE.*

*NOLI EX LIBRO PAGINAM ERIPERE.*

HOW SCANDALIZING TO VANDALIZE A BOOK.

NEVER TEAR PAGES FROM BOOKS.

---

Sophie wandered the halls of Gruffud's after classes had ended, her thoughts returning to what she'd seen in Minister Skelch's office. Last night, she had tried to tell Aunt Rue and Aunt Violet her suspicions about the Minister.

But Aunt Rue had only shaken her head. "What a wild imagination, my girl!" And Aunt Violet had shut herself in her room with her tea leaves.

Sophie had tried to sneak into her father's study to look through some of his books, but the door was shut, and Aunt Rue had given her one of her *looks* when she went near it.

Sophie stopped by Portia and Portius, hoping to tell them what she had seen in the Minister's office, but they were discussing snapdragon champions with Mage Quartz. The favourites seemed to be Godfrey

Whistler from North Dakota and Sedric Björnsson from Iceland. Sophie left them arguing heatedly about whether the local hero was Pierre Desjarlais from St. Laurent Island or Francesca Pazzolini from MiddleGate.

Guess I'll go to the library, she thought. Maybe Miss Heese can help me find out more about the Serpent's Chain; but Miss Heese was brainstorming with Sygnithia Sly about her pesky plant pest project for Mage Radix.

"My sloughworms are the biggest ones in the class, Miss Heese," bragged Sygnithia.

"How interesting, Miss Sly. Did you see the latest article in *Magic Today*? A whole spread on sloughworms—*Vermis luteus*, originally from Indonesia. What species of sloughworm are you studying in particular?"

Sophie muttered, "How could anyone be interested in sloughworms? Either way you pronounce it, slooworms or slufworms—" Her voice raised a notch. "—they're disgusting, swampy, limp things that do nothing except eat, moult and excrete!"

Miss Heese looked over at Sophie, her lips pursed. "May we remind you to keep your voice muted, Miss Isidor. We will be with you in a moment."

"Eat, moult and excrete...perfect for Sygnithia," muttered Sophie, while she scanned the shelves for books that might have something on the Serpent's Chain. She now had a stack of at least twenty volumes on the table. There's got to be something in one of these, she thought as she plopped the last three books down.

She picked up *The Sorcerer's Sourcebook of Magical Names* first, but it turned out to be a book of baby names. Then she turned to "Serpent's Chain" in *The Ultimate Compendium of Magykal Knowledge*. But the pages were torn out.

Quickly, she opened another book—*Magical Symbols, Rites and Passages*. "That's strange," she murmured. "This one's ripped out too!"

"What are you doing, Sophie? You look like you're taking out the whole library," said Merrily Klimchak, who had packed up her bags and was ready to leave.

"Um, I've got a special project," said Sophie, trying to think quickly, "something I'm working on for...for Mage Tibor—you know, to do with portals."

"He's obsessed with those things," said Merrily, shaking her head at the heap of books surrounding Sophie. "Glad it's not me."

"What do you seek?" said a voice in Sophie's left ear. "I dare say I should know all the books in this library."

"Hi, Peerslie," said Sophie. "Maybe *you* can help me. Can you believe someone's been ripping out the pages from these books?"

"Ghostie pages?" said Peerslie, his voice hovering somewhere above her head. Several pages of the open book on the table flipped over, as if by themselves.

"I'm looking for information about the Serpent's Chain," said Sophie.

The air turned icy cold, as if a door had opened and wintery air were blasting in.

"The Ch-Chaine of the Serpents?" said Peerslie, spluttering.

"Yes, that's right," said Sophie eagerly. She gazed up at the spot where she thought Peerslie was hovering. "Peerslie, are you there? Peerslie?"

Peerslie, if he were still there, said nothing.

Unnerving how he comes and goes, she thought. Always there when you wish he'd go away, and gone when you need him. But the air had turned icy when she asked him about the Serpent's Chain—as if he were scared.

She turned back to the book she was holding, which happened to be *The Big Book of Magyk and Beasts*. There were ten whole pages gone—all the way from "Salamanders" straight through to "Spiders." Someone must have been tearing out all these pages on purpose. "I've got to tell Miss Heese," she muttered. Carrying *The Big Book of Magyk and Beasts*, she walked over to the counter.

Sygnithia had long since left the library, and Miss Heese was nowhere to be seen. Sophie picked up the small silver bell and rang it.

At the sound of the bell, Miss Heese hurried out from a back room behind the counter. She removed a pair of white cotton gloves from her hands. "What can we do for you, Miss Isidor?"

"Miss Heese, I've been looking for information on the Serpent's Chain, but all the pages have been torn out."

"Pages torn? What are you talking about? Rule No. 3—No Tearing Pages from the Books!"

"Yes, I know, Miss Heese. It's just that...see for yourself." Sophie showed Miss Heese *The Big Book of Magyk and Beasts*. "The books are all ripped out right at *S-E-R-P*."

At the sight of all the ripped pages, Miss Heese's fluffy hair seemed to stand on end. "Who would have done such a thing?" She looked at Sophie suspiciously "Wait until I tell Mage Agassiz."

"But I need to find out what the Serpent's Chain is, Miss Heese."

Miss Heese, however, appeared to be beyond answering questions. She glared at Sophie, snatched the book from her and and stroked its cover.

Sophie wandered back to her table, feeling disconsolate. She probably thinks I ripped the pages out on purpose. She was holding that book like it was a baby, and now I'm no further ahead than before. She leafed through *Forgotten Magic*; it too was ripped, but there was the shred of a sentence left.

> *The Serpent's Chain was a secret society during the Middle Ages, the origins of which are shrouded—*

But she already knew that much from the book in her father's study.

Tap...tap...tap.

Where was that sound coming from? "Peerslie up to his old tricks," she murmured and turned back to the pile of books.

Tap...tap...tap.

That sounded like it was coming from really close by. Sophie glanced under the table. Her eyes widened; the carpet was lifting up all by itself!

I've never seen Peerslie do that, thought Sophie. She looked around to make sure no one else had noticed. Then she bent down and lifted up the corner of the carpet. There was a small door underneath—a trap door. She tapped on the door two times.

Two small knocks answered.

Sophie tapped again three times.

Three knocks answered.

"Help!" said a muffled voice.

The trapdoor rattled. Sophie looked around again to see if anyone else had noticed, but it was near closing time and the library was almost deserted. She lifted up the round iron ring on the trap door; stale air whooshed into the library.

"Who's th-th-there?" Sophie whispered.

"Help—I'm trapped," said the muffled voice.

"Who are you? What are you doing d-down there?" asked Sophie, her voice shaking.

"It's Wil—Wil Wychwood."

"Wil!" Sophie barely managed to stifle a shriek.

Wil's face, pale and drawn, looked out from under the trap door. His eyes blinked in the light.

"He'll come back any moment," said Wil in a panicked voice.

"Quick, come on." Sophie helped pull Wil up, closed the door and put the carpet back. "Stay under the table, so no one sees you."

"I could hear chairs scraping, and dust was falling through cracks in the ceiling," said Wil, his voice hoarse. "I crawled on top of a chair, and I could see a sort of door there with the light from the medallion."

"I thought you were Peeping Peerslie!" whispered Sophie. "I've been trying to find out more about the Serpent's Chain. Peeping Peerslie must know something because when I asked him about the Serpent's Chain, the air turned icy cold and he took off.

"And I searched Minister Skelch's office, but he suddenly appeared out of nowhere, so I had to leave. The only thing I found was his cloak—the one he wore when he was Snow King. It had a big rip in the back. And there was a jar with an eye in it sitting right on his desk and blue jewels everywhere. I've got a whole handful of them in my pocket." Sophie stopped to take a breath and looked around.

The library was completely empty now, and Miss Heese must have been doing something in her back office.

Wil fumbled at his pocket and pulled out the black medallion and gold ring from his jacket. "I hid the medallion and he got really angry."

"Who's he?" whispered Sophie.

"I don't know who," said Wil.

"Do you think it was Minister Skelch?"

"Maybe."

"It must be Minister Skelch. Who else could it be? You were right all along."

Sophie stared down at Wil's hand. "Where did you get those?"

Together with the medallion, Wil was holding...blue jewels.

"Storage room," said Wil in a trembling voice.

"They must have come from Minister Skelch's cloak," whispered Sophie. "Take my arm. Portia and Portius will be taking their afternoon nap. We'll sneak by them."

---

One of Portia's snake braids twitched, causing Portia to open one eye. She hummed, "Ah, he is found, who was lost."

# XXXVI Welcome News

*How can soggy leaves foretell the future?*

---

*SI SAPO VILIS EST, BULLAE TENUES SUNT.*

**IF THE SOAP BE CHEAP, THE BUBBLES BE THIN.**

---

"Sophie, turn the radio on. We'll catch the news, dear," said Aunt Violet. She shooed Cadmus off the kitchen counter and waved at two long-handled spoons stirring a pot of stew on the stove by themselves. Then she stared down at the dishes clattering in the sink and frowned. "What is the matter with this soap?"

Sophie turned the knob on the radio, and a loud voice intruded upon the clatter.

"—shank, a slippery figure in the shadowy underworld, and a master of disguise. A warrant for his arrest has been issued.

"Now, for all our listeners, do you know what day it is today? Yes, February 2nd, Alphonse Lisquatch's seventy-fifth birthday. Alphonse Lisquatch—the man who invented snow candy and holds patents in forty-three countries. Winterlude wouldn't be the same without it! It's also," the voice crooned, "Shadow Day! If groundhogs see their shadow today, they pop back into their holes for six more weeks of winter weather. If they don't see it, spring's coming soon!"

"We must have missed the rest of the news. Just turn it off, Sophie," said Aunt Violet, sounding impatient. She pointed at the dishes in the sink. "Mind yourselves. No breaking."

"If I were a groundhog, I wouldn't even poke my nose out, it's so cold," said Sophie, looking at the blustery winds outside.

———ɔʰɔ———

When Wil came down for breakfast, Aunt Violet threw him a soapy kiss through the air.

"Did you see your letter, dear?" she asked. "It came in this morning's mail. Sophie, where's that letter to Wil?"

"Who was it from, Aunt Violet?" asked Wil.

"Why, from Mr. Bertram. It will be nice to see Bartholomew again. It's been years, since Cyril—" Aunt Violet broke off, and started the dishes jostling furiously in the sink.

Mr. Bertram—coming to MiddleGate? Wil could hardly believe his ears.

"Cadmus," scolded Sophie, "you're sitting on the letter, just to tease everyone."

The corner of an envelope was peeking out from underneath Cadmus. Sophie snatched up the envelope and danced around the table, holding the envelope high in the air.

"That's mine," said Wil, chasing after her.

"What will you give me for it?"

"Sophie, give Wil his letter, dear."

Sophie only laughed, but Wil grabbed at the letter and there was an awful, ripping sound.

"Look what you've done," Aunt Violet said, her voice ominous. "Bad luck to rip a letter!"

Wil pulled out two halves of a letter from the envelope. There was Mr. Bertram's writing.

"Read it, Wil. I want to hear. Is Mr. Bertram coming? I've never met him before—have I, Aunt Violet?" asked Sophie.

"Hmmm, dear?" said Aunt Violet, sounding preoccupied.

Wil skimmed the last few lines of the letter.

*The shop is just not the same without you and Esme. I plan to visit MiddleGate this spring. It's years since I've seen the Narcisse Play, and perhaps we'll take a trip to the Narcisse caves too.*

*Yours truly,*

*B. Bertram*

"Aunt Violet, how did you know?" asked Wil, looking up from the letter.

"How did I what?" replied Aunt Violet, looking up from the dishes. Small soap bubbles were floating all over the kitchen, and a huge one was hanging from her chin. It popped as she said, "They promised me at Quigley's Market that the dishes would practically fly out of the water themselves, spanking clean. Don't believe a word of it."

Wil supposed Aunt Violet had been studying tea leaves again. But how could soggy leaves foretell the future?

His grandmother would have waved her hands. *That's pure nonsense, William. Wishful thinking and party games, nothing more.*

But Mr. Bertram was coming. That was all that mattered. He'd never imagined Mr. Bertram would know how to find MiddleGate.

# XXXVII Strange Dream

*The creature sank to the bottom.*

---

*SOMNIA INCERTA SUNT. QUID DICANT—*
*PRAETERITA, PRAESENTIA, FUTURA VEL NUMQUAM?*

DREAMS ARE CONFUSING.
DO THEY SPEAK ABOUT WAS, IS, WILL OR NEVER?

---

Wil jostled into his place on the grade-five benches in Stone Hall. Mage Agassiz started with the morning matins' general announcements. "Every three years, Gruffud's puts on a shadow play in the springtime. It is one of the highlights of the school year, and students spend many hours preparing..."

Wil shifted on the bench and tugged at his uniform, which had bunched up somehow. He felt a tiny lump in his pocket and brought out whatever it was—a blue jewel from the Snow King's costume. He couldn't believe three months had already gone by since he'd been trapped in that dark storage room.

Ever since then, he'd been treated as a bit of a hero at Gruffud's. Jinzhen Cheng had offered to let Wil try out his new invisible-ink pen any time he wanted to, and Maia and Meena Amorante, had begged him to join the S.O.S. Club—the Save our Serpents Club—which met once a week after school. Not wanting to hurt their feelings, he had gone to two or three meetings, but found that he got a headache whenever they began talking acronyms.

He knew A.D.D.E.R was the Association for the Destruction and Disposal of Evil Reptiles. I.S.N.O.G—the International Snakes No! Guild, another radical group that hated snakes. After that, there was R.E.D.—something about reptiles and the environment. S.N.A.K.E., N.A.S.S.U.S., U.N.I.S.E.R.P., The Society for the Protection of Magical Creatures Liable to Vivisection, The Society of the Friends of the Rights of Serpents. He counted on his fingers. That was eight; no, it was nine. There was also The Snake Club, and the Society of the Serpentine Way. That made eleven. Weren't there two more? Everyone else seemed to know all the names, but he couldn't keep them all straight.

Peeping Peerslie had made it difficult to do any work in the library since Wil's kidnapping—he kept hovering around, making suggestions about Wil's homework, as if afraid that Wil might disappear again. One afternoon, Wil had complained, "Peerslie, *please*. This is *my* homework. Go do your *own*."

Peerslie wailed, "But I don't have any homework." With a sharp crackle and pop, Peerslie had banished himself from the library for two whole days. When Peerslie had finally returned, Wil had actually been glad to see—or rather hear—him again; he even found himself offering to get extra copies of homework for Peerslie.

Peerslie had been so pleased at the offer he spent the rest of the afternoon bothering everyone in the library—switching pens, turning pages when they weren't looking, returning books to the shelves when they hadn't finished with them yet, adding up sums incorrectly, leading someone on a wild goose chase through the whole library, filling in the blanks on question sheets, hiding assignments from their owners. Wil had had to leave the library to get any work done by himself.

Miss Heese flitted protectively over Wil and Sophie, as if Wil were about to be kidnapped again. She saved them special books—for Wil, the *Frobishmead Magic* series by Conrad Silver, about a young boy who could transform into a snake and got into all kinds of mischief; and for Sophie, a collection of drawings by Ishbel Montagu, renowned for her illustrations of imaginary creatures. The drawings were so lifelike, it was whispered that her drawings actually *could* come to life. Sophie studied Montagu's work for hours on end, until Wil dragged her home for supper.

**137**

Miss Heese had even stopped harping about rules. She must have felt it was *her* fault that Wil had been locked in the basement of the library. Whatever the reason, Wil actually missed her terse "Rule No. 1, No Noise that came but infrequently now."

And he had finally met the Firecatchers. They wore long, red cloaks and hoods so that he couldn't see their faces, just as Sophie had said, and they emanated bitter smoke, which eddied about his head. It had felt as if they were trying to probe inside his skull, to pull something out from him that he didn't want them to know—a disagreeable sensation. He had said nothing to them about the black medallion or the gold ring—both of them had been nestled in his pocket—afraid they might take them away.

No one asked him any more questions after that, and everything was almost back to normal—if you didn't count the fact that nine Firecatchers had been posted to Gruffud's, much to Portia and Portius's chagrin. It was impossible not to see the Firecatchers wherever you went, and lessons were frequently in a shambles, for whoever passed by the Firecatchers' smoke could hardly think straight afterwards. There was no help for it, though, as many parents had threatened to pull their children from Gruffud's without some guarantee of their children's safety. Mage Aggasiz had been hard pressed to deal with the unfavourable press, the worst of which suggested one of the Gruffud's very own teachers must have been responsible for Wil's kidnapping.

Wil overheard Portia complaining to Portius the morning the Firecatchers arrived.

"In all our years—such a lack of trust."

"Now, Portia, my dear," said Portius in a soothing voice. "It's for the good of the school. It can't hurt to have the Firecatchers on guard too."

"We've been protecting Gruffud's for four hundred and ninety-four years." Portia sniffed. "You'd think that would count for something."

Four hundred and ninety-four years? Portia and Portius must have come from the original school in Britain, thought Wil.

"Portia," said Portius, his voice harsh, "remember the time of the Persecutions and the Burning Wall Revolt."

Portia had closed her eyes at Portius's words and refused to speak any further.

With the prospect of Mr. Bertram coming, though, Wil's memories of being knocked out in ditchball, hiding the black medallion and gold ring from his captor and being kidnapped for two whole days—all these faded in importance.

But last night—last night he had had a strange dream. A long, brown snake slithered up from a hole in the ground. It followed him no matter which way he turned. He fell on the ground and was sure that the snake would catch him. But someone—he didn't know who—nabbed the snake and held it up in the air. The snake whipped from side to side, looking desperate; it became small, like a little salamander no longer than three or four inches. It had a human face, two legs, and two arms tinged with soft brown fur. The someone—whoever it was—dropped the creature into a glass beaker of water. It sank to the bottom of the beaker, struggling to breathe. Its tiny hands convulsed several times, and then uncurled... one...last...time. Wil had awoken from the dream feeling lost and sad.

At he thought of those tiny furry hands clenching and unclenching, Wil drew the sleeve of his uniform across his nose, and tried to concentrate on Mage Agassiz's words.

"—great honour to be chosen. According to tradition, a name will now be drawn. The lucky person will choose a friend to help him or her."

"What's she doing?" whispered Wil to Olin Cramer, who happened to be sitting beside him.

"She's picking a name, can't you see?" said Olin.

Wil didn't dare ask for what, because Stone Hall had gone completely quiet.

Mage Terpsy stepped up to the front. She was holding a polished silver bowl with two winged serpents on either side. Holding the bowl out, she drew it in a circle three times, then placed it on the table in front of her.

The bowl gleamed in the dimness of Stone Hall and Wil craned his neck to see what would happen next.

Mage Agassiz put her hand into the silver bowl and withdrew a piece of paper. She unfolded it, and frowned. "There seems to have been a mistake. This paper is blank."

Loud whispers broke out in the hall. "That's a bad sign, isn't it?" "Does that mean we can't do the play this year?"

Mage Agassiz turned to Mage Adderson and asked her a question, but Mage Adderson merely shook her head. Mage Agassiz nodded to Mage Terpsy, who picked the sphere up and again drew it three times through the air.

Mage Agassiz pulled out another piece of paper, unfolded it and smiled.

"We are pleased to announce that William Wychwood, one of our new grade fives, will be serving on the Committee this year. William, please step forward to accept this honour."

Wil was stunned.

What Committee?

Everyone was clapping, and there was a loud buzzing sound in his head. He made his way to the front, and Mage Agassiz handed him a huge stack of papers more than a foot high tied round with red ribbon.

# XXXVIII The Box

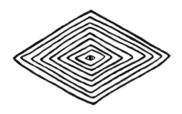

*What's inside?*

---

*LICET INCOGNITA COGNOSCERE?*

THE UNKNOWABLE—WHAT CANNOT BE ASKED.

---

Wil and Sophie were sprawled on the living room floor, reading through a stack of plays and munching on ginger cookies. The grandfather clock chimed four.

"Listen to this: 'Come back, you scoundrel. Return my wig at once.'" Sophie broke into giggles.

"Careful. Keep everything in order," said Wil.

"Don't be so grumpy," said Sophie, and she bit into another cookie. "This one might be good," she said, as she leafed through another play. "Lots of disguises...big fight at the end."

"What's the title?" asked Wil.

"*The Elixir of Youth*," Sophie replied.

"Yeah, I looked at that one. Too many characters." Wil held up a yellowed copy of another play. "What about this one? It's called *The Box.*"

"What's it about?" asked Sophie.

"It's about a box, what do you think?" said Wil. "No really, it's like a dream I had...peeling away layers of paper; there was always another one underneath."

"Like an onion?" asked Sophie.

"Yeah," said Wil. "Here's what it says."

*Fifteen hundred years ago, three thin documents were placed inside a box. Wedding documents? Special poems? Letters? The box was sewn in silk cloth. Over the centuries, the box was placed inside seven more boxes, each larger than the last and sewn in cloth. Four hundred years ago, the box was placed inside yet one more box with a note of warning sewn to the outside*—Open This Not or Suffer the Consequences. *Three hundred years ago, the eighth box was placed inside a ninth box. The warning was repeated.*

"So, did they open them?" asked Sophie.

"Not right away," said Wil. "The box was lost for many years, but then someone found it in a dusty storage cabinet. They decided to open the boxes, one by one, even with the warnings. They reached the last box; and a huge argument broke out. Someone wanted to open the last box, but the others didn't. In the middle of the night, someone snuck into the chamber where the box sat on a pedestal...but he was caught. It was decided once and for all not to open the box—leaving its contents still a mystery."

"I'd want to know what's inside, wouldn't you?" asked Sophie.

"Maybe there's something awful in there, and everyone would regret opening it, but it would be too late," said Wil.

"First, too many characters. Next, too many boxes," said Sophie, breaking into giggles again.

"You're probably right," said Wil, his shoulders sagging. He looked out the window at the dark clouds scudding across the bleak winter sky.

The grandfather clock chimed five.

My luck to get picked anyway and to have to read all these plays, he thought.

# XXXIX  The Committee's Decision

*Should we open the last one?*

---

*IUVENES SENECTUTEM NON SOLLICITANT.*
THE YOUNG DON'T WORRY ABOUT GROWING OLD.

---

Wil stood fidgeting with his sash in Gruffud's Office beneath the twelve portraits of past principals—they were all dressed in colourful robes and each was holding an open book. Wil felt as if they were staring at him, wondering who he was.

Two people were opening the morning mail, and several others were riffling through tall stacks of files; but no one seemed to notice him standing by the counter.

Wil looked around for a bell. As there was none, he cleared his throat.

One of the women looked up. "Yes? May I help you?" she asked.

"I'm...I'm here for the Shadow Play Committee meeting," said Wil, feeling tongue-tied.

The woman smiled and pointed to spiral stairs at the back of the office. "Mage Agassiz's office is at the top of the stairs."

As soon as he stepped on the wooden stairs and held the handrail, the stairs began to circle silently upwards—like an escalator. A coiled serpent with an eagle's head carved in dark wood crouched at the top of the banister on the landing.

Where was the door to Mage Agassiz's office?

There was only a large painting of Gruffud's Academy—only it wasn't Gruffud's. The trees looked different and the big stone in front was missing, but the clock tower was the same.

Wil looked at the coiled eagle serpent again. Its knobbly backbones were worn away by what must have been the touch of hundreds of students over the years. He wondered if it had come from the original Gruffud's, like Portia and Portius—and perhaps that was the old school in the painting. He ran his fingers over the creature's spine. To Wil's surprise, the eagle serpent's sightless eyes glistened and turned amber with a black slit pupil. The eyes gazed steadily at Wil, and then the painting swung out from the wall, leading to a large room beyond. He heard a voice coming from behind a tall-backed chair.

"...great honour to join the Committee. I certainly remember my first performance, even though I played only a very small part."

Wil recognized that voice. It belonged to Mrs. Blancheflour, whom he had met—if met was the right word—in the egg shop the day of the blue egg fiasco. He stopped at the doorway, his heart pounding, and glanced around the room.

Mage Agassiz's office was lined in bookcases and tall cabinets filled with jars, clocks and strange devices. Mage Agassiz, Mage Tibor, Miss Heese and Mage Terpsy were already sitting at a long oak table, surrounded by piles of paper.

"Welcome, Mr. Wychwood," said Mage Agassiz, gesturing for Wil to sit beside her. "William Wychwood is our student representative this year on the Committee, Mrs. Blancheflour. And Mrs. Blancheflour is the President of the Narcisse Society."

With these introductions completed, Mrs. Blancheflour beamed at Wil and held out her hand to shake his.

Would she remember the day the blue egg broke...and that it had been his fault?

But Mrs. Blancheflour seemed not to have the faintest recollection.

"Just Minister Skelch still to come." Mage Agassiz glanced over to a clock by the window.

Not Minister Skelch! thought Wil with a rush of anger. No one had told him that the Minister was on the Committee too. He hadn't seen the Minister since Winterlude's ditchball game. But it made sense. Mrs. Blancheflour was the President of the Narcisse Society, which always sponsored the play, and the Minister was responsible for the Narcisse snakes.

"So sorry to be tardy—not my usual way of doing business," said Minister Skelch as he breezed into the office and flung his coat on a chair by the door.

What a liar. He's always late, thought Wil. He stared at the Minister, more sure than ever that he was somehow involved in the killing of the Narcisse snakes.

"Minister Skelch and Mrs. Blancheflour, thank you for taking time from your busy schedules to be with us today," said Mage Agassiz. "I hope you've all had a chance to review the plays and have picked your favourite. I'm sure this year's production will be one of the best yet. As Chair of the Shadow Play Committee, I do not vote, except to break a tie." Mage Agassiz smiled and gazed around the table expectantly.

Minister Skelch was the first to speak. "Without stealing anyone's thunder, *The Snow King* adaptation was my personal favourite."

Without acknowledging what the Minister had just said, Miss Heese held up a sheaf of papers. "We think this quest story, *The Elixir of Youth*, was very interesting—surely a theme with universal appeal."

"Yes, life eternal—the holy grail." Mrs. Blancheflour nodded her head vigorously.

"Mrs. Blancheflour and Miss Heese, with all due respect, surely that play would only appeal to those getting on in years, rather than those who are in the prime of that sacred state of childhood." Minister Skelch bowed in Wil's direction. Then he turned back to Miss Heese. "I didn't worry about growing old when I was young; did you?"

Miss Heese's dandelion hair seemed to bristle for a moment.

"Well, I think we should be supporting our local talent. Martine Godsey's play was a delight—" said Mage Terpsy.

"If we can't...hmmm, discuss this in a civilized fashion—" interrupted Mage Tibor.

"But *The Snow King* was written by a Gruffud graduate—" protested Minister Skelch.

"It's clear to me that certain people are...hmmm, unprepared for any meaningful discussion—" Mage Tibor continued.

"Are we to understand that no one is interested in—" said Miss Heese.

Wil began to lose track of who was saying what.

"But I hated that one." "We can't always get what we want." "I think that one would be my last choice."

Someone slammed a bundle of papers onto the table. Startled, Wil knocked against Mage Tibor's pile of papers, which splayed all over the floor.

Mage Agassiz cleared her throat, and spoke in an even voice with only the barest hint of vexation. "Understandably, Gruffud's Academy wishes to tackle only the best. We pride ourselves on our shadow plays." She paused and turned to Wil. "Mr. Wychwood, as our student representative, do you have any suggestions for the Selection Committee?"

All faces turned to Wil at the same time. In the silence that followed, he had to think quickly.

Skelch's choice of *The Snow King* was a little selfish. And Miss Heese and Mrs. Blancheflour wanted everlasting youth, but *The Elixir of Youth* had too many characters and disguises—it was confusing. And why did Miss Heese keep saying "we" as though everybody agreed with her?

Everyone was waiting; he had to say something.

"Um...I...I...thought—"

"Feel free to speak," said Mage Agassiz. "All voices are equal on this matter."

"The one...the one about the box," said Wil.

"I don't recall that one. Was that in the material we were given?" asked Mrs. Blancheflour.

The others didn't answer her. They were all looking curiously at Wil.

"It's talking about mysteries...things we can't know...and won't ever know," said Wil, his voice getting smaller and smaller.

No one said a word at first. Then the clamour of voices erupted again.

"Good idea," said Miss Heese, "even though we're still partial to *The Elixir of Eternal Youth*."

"*The Box*—interesting idea," said Mage Tibor.

At the same time Mage Terpsy said, "I think *The Box* is a good choice, myself."

"Yes, yes, profound—the Unknowable—That Which Cannot Be Asked," said Minister Skelch. "There are some good scenes—the ones where they're arguing about whether or not to open the box. Good dramatic conflict there."

"Oh, yes, here it is—was right here all the time," said Mrs. Blancheflour in a loud voice, and she waved a yellowed, dog-eared copy of *The Box* in the air.

# XL  Final Dress Rehearsal

*The dragon Greed.*

The snows had melted at least a month ago; it was a cool spring day threatening rain at the beginning of May. These days, Sophie and Wil had scarcely enough time to do homework or study for June exams, let alone wonder why Wil's kidnapper had wanted the black medallion—for they had been rehearsing the shadow play several times a week.

The shadow puppets were made from thin, rigid cardboard punched with small holes. The players knelt behind a large cloth screen lit by phosphoworm lanterns; they held the shadow puppets on long poles, while the members of the choir stood in the pit in front of the stage. The audience would never see the puppets themselves, just the shadows they cast on the screen.

Most of the play's juicy parts had been taken by older students, who had all started out in the same way as Sophie and Wil—handing the puppets to the players, storing the puppets back in their boxes, moving props and scenery about, and making sure the phosphoworms were properly fed so they glowed brightly. This last was no task for the timid, as Sophie had soon found out. The phosphoworms were grumpy unless they were fed greens regularly; it was easy to be nipped by one.

After having hauled everything out of her locker to find a library book—and not finding it—Sophie was late for the morning's final dress rehearsal. The benches in Stone Hall had been moved to the side, and the chandeliers overhead swayed imperceptibly as Mr. and Mrs. Pyper finished polishing the floor to a high sheen. Sophie had never had a clear view of the floor in Stone Hall before and was surprised to see a black and white stone labyrinth on the floor—it was a square-cornered snake with the tail as the entrance and the head at its centre.

Loud voices were arguing behind the yellow parchment screen at the front of Stone Hall.

"Move over, can't you? You're taking up the whole stage."

"Where do you want me to move to? There's nowhere else to go!"

"Please, please everyone!" said Mage Terpsy. She tapped the baton on the podium. "Hiss and lear, everyone. This is not going to work, unless everyone is in their places. It's already a quarter past the hour, and we haven't even begun our dress rehearsal." Her voice rose. "And please make an effort to be on time!" She glared at Sophie.

Sophie ducked her head. "Sorry, Mage Terpsy. I won't let it happen again."

"There won't be much opportunity for *again*, will there Miss Isidor, given the fact that we perform in just a hew flours!" said Mage Terpsy. She tapped the baton impatiently on the podium.

"You nervous?" whispered Wil to Sophie as she crouched down behind the screen.

Sophie shook her head. "It's not like we're holding the puppets, you know. I have to run home after rehearsal to get a library book. I must have left it on the kitchen table and it's due today. Miss Heese will kill me."

"Chorus puppets, ready yourselves!" said Mage Terpsy, tapping the baton so loudly that Sophie thought it would snap in half. "We'll start at the beginning of Act III."

Mage Terpsy's baton fell, and soprano voices soared into the air, sending shivers down Sophie's spine.

Sophie watched one of the grade tens, Stephan Lorimer, holding the shadow puppet of the dragon Greed, which Wil had just passed to him. Greed marched across the screen towards the Elders, a group of old, stooped sages huddled around a box.

The choir broke into shrill keening.

Stephan's too close to the screen, thought Sophie.

"Stop, stop!" Mage Terpsy tapped on the podium again with the baton. "The choir—nary vice work. But we must start again, I'm afraid.

"Stephan, you're much too close to the screen. Remember, the shadows are too small when you're so close. The shadow of Greed must be large.

"No, no, you're too far away now—that shadow is much, much too big." Mage Terpsy rubbed the side of her head, as if she had a headache.

Sophie turned back to inspect the phosphoworm lanterns. The phosphoworms were munching happily on lettuce leaves; their light cast clear, dark shadows on the screen. One of the other grade tens, though, was having trouble keeping her balance, and her puppet's shadow was definitely wobbling.

"Extend your arms, up and up, the music rises," said Mage Terpsy, her voice becoming more frantic by the moment. "Yes, this is the moment! The poxes are biled one on top of the other."

Sophie touched her ear—the special signal she and Wil used every time Mage Terpsy mixed up her letters. But Wil had already pulled out his small notebook and was adding *hew flours, nary vice* and *biled poxes*—that last one had to be one of the best—to his ever-growing list of *tipsy-terpsies*.

"Good, good...mind they don't topple—not yet!" exclaimed Mage Terpsy. "Watch, one of the shadows is wobbling. Please, it's very distracting. Puppeteers, hold yourselves steady. All right, one more time."

Mage Terpsy raised the baton, but at the sound of a slight commotion at the back of the hall, she turned around, looking annoyed. "One moment please, everyone."

Sophie looked out from behind the screen to see a Firecatcher sweeping into the Hall. Why was a Firecatcher interested in their dress rehearsal? Although Sophie couldn't hear what Mage Terpsy was saying, her voice and gestures grew more and more animated. She must have been trying to persuade the Firecatcher to let them rehearse in peace.

Mage Terpsy strode back towards the stage, fretting, "...not right with the Firecatchers about, when we're trying to get ready for the play. How can one think straight?" She drew the baton out from her pocket. "Again, please, from the top of Act III!"

"Wil, Stefan needs Greed," whispered Sophie to Wil, who seemed to be busy counting the *tipsy-terpsies* in his small notebook. "We're starting from the top of Act III again."

Wil threw the notebook down and scrambled to hand Greed to Stefan, but tripped over the rod of another puppet, which had been left lying on the floor. Wil pitched into the screen, and with a great crash, fell off the stage right into the choir pit—narrowly missing three of the sopranos.

"Mr. Wychwood, are you all right?" asked Mage Terpsy, who looked as if she were about to cry.

Obviously still trying to catch his breath, Wil nodded without saying a word.

"Everyone, please help Mr. Wychwood up." Terpsy sighed and shook her head. "Let's check the damage."

The puppet Greed was thankfully intact; even the screen had suffered no harm.

"They do say a great performance follows a dour press rehearsal. Let us hope so," said Mage Terpsy, her expression and voice both grim.

*Dour press rehearsal*—she must have meant poor dress rehearsal, thought Sophie. She looked over at Wil, who was still lying on the floor and looking dazed. He touched his ear.

Sophie grabbed Wil's small notebook and jotted the latest *tipsy-terpsie* down. We must have more than a hundred already! she thought.

# XLI The Manuscript

*The S turned instantly into two coiling, snake-like creatures.*

---

*QUOD INVENIAS SUB CATTO DORMIENTE NUMQUAM NESCIS.*
YOU NEVER KNOW WHAT YOU'LL FIND
UNDERNEATH A SLEEPING CAT.

---

Sophie shook out her wet hair and wiped the raindrops from her eyeglasses. "Cadmus, I'm home. Are you snoozing somewhere?"

The house was quiet but for the ticking of the grandfather's clock. The clock stood as tall as the ceiling; on its face, the sun and moon watched over the Earth, surrounded by the planets and stars. The sun and the moon used to turn, but one day they had simply frozen in place. Now they were grinning down at her—both stuck halfway across the heavens.

Sophie picked up *A History of Gruffud's*, which was still lying on the breakfast table, and nibbled at a ginger cookie. She stood by the window and watched the gargoyle shake its tail dry, as the sun peeped out from behind a cloud.

"Maybe there'll be a rainbow," she said. "Cadmus, where are you? I bet you're sleeping upstairs in my closet."

She turned towards the stairs, but noticed the door of the study was ajar. There was the sound of purring from within.

"Cadmus, you're in big trouble." Sophie peered around the study door.

Stretched out on top of Cyril Isidor's papers, Cadmus was basking in a burst of sun's rays.

"Cadmus, get off, you bad cat!"

Cadmus yawned and stretched, as if he knew Sophie weren't really angry. When she scratched him under his chin, he purred more loudly and knocked against a pair of gold-rimmed eyeglasses on the desk. Sophie tried them on; everything was bent, distorted. She replaced the eyeglasses on the desk, and her eyes lit on the glint of gold leaf on a manuscript.

"What are you sitting on, old cat?" Sophie pushed Cadmus off the manuscript, and dust rose into the air; she sneezed.

Startled by the loud noise, Cadmus jumped off the desk, and a piece of paper fluttered to the floor.

"Sorry, Cadmus," said Sophie. She picked up the piece of paper— it was a half-finished letter. She wondered if it had been written by her father. Feeling a little as if she were trespassing, she read it intently. It was written to someone named Bart and ended with

> ..."umbra nullam umbram facit" *translates as "a shadow has no shadow," or "a shadow casts no shadow." I'm dismayed we haven't cracked the code yet. The coiling serpents illumination is so vivid. I am certain it is the key to another gate out—*

Here the letter ended abruptly.

Sophie looked at the gold-leafed letter *S* in the top left corner of the manuscript; the *S* was followed by scrambled words. What did they mean? Without stopping to think that students weren't supposed to do magic outside Gruffud's, she drew a circle in the air counter-clockwise and murmured "*Mixusfixus*," hoping the letters would turn into clear words. Instead, the *S* turned instantly into two coiling, snake-like creatures.

# XLII Memories

*Tempus fugit.*

---

*AUDE SAPERE, SED NOLI ABUTI QUO SCIS.*

DARE TO BE WISE, BUT DO NOT ABUSE YOUR KNOWLEDGE.

---

Jostled by the rhythmic chugging of the train and feeling sleepy, Mr. Bertram put down *The Life of Xiphia Tartarus*...not as promising as he had hoped, given the mage philosopher's fame. Her theories about simultaneous transformational dimensionality had changed the magical world's ideas about elemental methodologies and indivisibilitarianism. The book was 747 pages long; but some pages were half-filled with foot-notes in small print—obscure references to Tartarus's sensational love affairs. Mr. Bertram shifted uncomfortably in his seat and glanced out the window at the greening fields of wheat. A fox was loping alongside the tracks in the waning afternoon light.

He should have made this trip home a long time ago, he thought. How many years has it been? Must be ten years if it were a day—much too long. Snake's pox! Who was that kicking the back of the seat? He turned around; there was a young woman, whose eyes were red-rimmed. She was holding a letter and staring out the window, with the look of someone who had lost her first true love. Embarrassed, Mr. Bertram looked away.

He got up, stretched his legs, then smiled to himself, thinking about Esme getting lost on the train. What a scene if must have been, judging by one of Will's letters.

He walked up and down the aisle. Yes, it was far too long. Had it really been ten years since Cyril had died, and left Rue and Aunt Violet to raise Sophie?

He, Cyril and Rufus—the three of them had been inseparable all through their years at Gruffud's. It must be more than twenty years since he'd seen Rufus. The last time would have been that spring pilgrimage to see the snakes of Narcisse.

But Rufus went his own way. He'd gotten interested in some of the more obscure arts—and they lost touch. But why mince words? Obscure meant dark. Mr. Bertram grimaced. Those were the magical arts that relied on fear and intimidation. They should never have been invented.

He and Cyril had tried to dissuade Rufus, but he had only laughed at them. It was the night of Gruffud's Halloween Masquerade Ball. They were wearing that old costume of the three-headed dog; he and Cyril got into a terrific fight with Rufus.

"We're not supposed to be learning that sort of incantation," Cyril said to Rufus.

"What sort of incantation?" asked Rufus, his eyes dangerously dark.

"Like forcing people to do things they don't want to do. You're messing with the black arts," Cyril said to Rufus, "Why are you being so stupid? Are you trying to get expelled?"

Mr. Bertram remembered how he had tried to intervene. "Rufus, we're your friends. Do you think we don't know you've been sneaking into the Library's Restricted Section?"

"Scared?" said Rufus, taunting them both. "You'll never get ahead. *Nihil obstat*—nothing stands in my way. You keep out of my business; I'll keep out of yours. If it were up to people like you who always want to censor everything..."

Rufus had torn off his dog's head and thrown it onto the floor. "You two can't even begin to understand."

The train swayed and Mr. Bertram almost lost his balance. He gained his footing and thought, what a pleasure it would be to see Wil again. He seemed to have fit right in at Gruffud's.

# XLIII Grunion Square

*...upside down into a roaring whirl of frozen air.*

---

*SEMPER DEPONE VESTIGIA.*

ALWAYS LEAVE A TRAIL BEHIND YOU.

---

Sophie walked back to Gruffud's hardly noticing the puddles, her mind spinning. What did those two coiling serpents on the manuscript mean? Her father had thought there was another gate out...a gate out of where? MiddleGate?

Sophie remembered the ink spilling over her map of MiddleGate in Mage Tibor's class...right on top of Grunion Square. Her heart quickened. What if the two coiling serpents were the Brimstone Snakes?

As she approached Grunion Square, she was surprised to see someone sitting on top of the Brimstone Snakes—it wasn't unusual to see someone perched there, but usually only children did that. Instead, this was someone wearing a long, black cloak with a hood.

Sophie crept behind one of the trees lining Grunion Square. The Brimstone Snakes glistened in the afternoon sun and steam was rising from their metal scales. Above their heads, a rainbow arched across the sky.

Sophie crept closer, and hid behind another tree. Edging closer still, she distinctly heard the person say in a hoarse voice, "*Umbra nullam umbram facit.*"

Those are the same words as in the letter, thought Sophie. Wait until I tell Wil about this...

At that moment, the person turned, looked right at her and—Sophie couldn't believe her eyes—vanished into thin air!

Sophie stepped out from behind the tree and looked all around the Brimstone Snakes. Whoever it was had disappeared without a trace. She looked up—now a double rainbow arched across the sky. She put her library book between two of the boulders where it was dry. Then she took out a piece of chalk from her pocket and wrote the words *umbra nullam umbram facit* on one of the stones at the base of the Brimstone Snakes; but the stone was wet and the chalk lines wobbled and caked.

Still trying to understand what she'd just seen, Sophie clambered to the top of the snake just as the afternoon bells began to ring at Gruffud's. Oh, now I'm late, she thought with a sinking heart. I'd better—

A rough hand clamped over Sophie's mouth.

"*Umbra nullam umbram facit,*" said a hoarse voice. "*Umbra nullam umbram facit. Umbra nullam umbram facit.*"

All of a sudden, Sophie felt herself pulled upside down into a roaring whirl of frozen air. She had only a moment to pull several blue jewels from her pocket and fling them.

# XLIV Shadow Play

*Can you trust a shadow?*

---

*FABULA AGENDA EST.*

THE SHOW MUST GO ON.

---

The phosphoworm lanterns were polished, the puppets lined up. Backstage was deadly quiet. Stephan Lorimer paced in the wings, refusing to talk with anyone. The chorus puppeteers, usually full of banter, stood at attention holding their puppets, not saying a word—not even looking at each other.

Wil crouched down, ready to take the hoods off the lanterns. He frowned and looked around. Where is Sophie? he wondered. It didn't take that long to go home.

"Places, everyone," said Mage Terpsy, bustling past. "Please check everything one last time. I know you'll do a splendid job."

"Mage Terpsy," Wil called out.

"Yes, Mr. Wychwood?"

"Sophie isn't here, Mage Terpsy."

"Of course she's here, Mr. Wychwood. She's probably just slipped out to the washroom—performance jitters, no doubt. Don't we all have those?" Mage Terpsy laughed nervously. "Skinister Melch is about to deliver the official welcome! Places, everyone!"

Wil felt the familiar lurch in his stomach every time he saw Minister Skelch or heard his name. He peeped around the screen; everyone was laughing and chatting.

Where were Aunt Rue and Aunt Violet?

Mr. Egbertine and Auguste were sitting beside each other. Auguste was talking animatedly to a young woman sitting in front of him, but she was looking at her programme and appeared not to be listening. And Mrs. Blancheflour was sitting in the front row beside Mr. Oystein. Wil looked for the snake's head cane, but this time, Mr. Oystein was carrying just an ordinary wood cane. At last, he spotted Aunt Rue and Aunt Violet. They were sitting ten rows from the front. And right beside them—Mr. Bertram! But Wil's pleasure at seeing Mr. Bertram was tempered by his worry about Sophie.

The lights dimmed and a hush grew over the crowd.

Mage Agassiz, wearing green velvet robes, strode onstage and bowed.

"Ladies and Gentlemen, welcome. Gruffud's Academy is proud to present our afternoon performance of the Narcisse Play, which celebrates the spring emergence of the snakes of Narcisse. Everyone is, of course, also welcome to attend our Saturday evening performance two days hence.

"I will call upon Minister Skelch to deliver the official welcome, in his roles as the Minister responsible for the safekeeping of the snakes of Narcisse and *ex officio* as a member of the Shadow Play Committee. Minister Skelch holds the Ninth Rank in the Order of the Snakes. He has also received the highest honour ever to be bestowed by the Order—the Caduceus Cross."

Mage Agassiz looked to her right and raised her hand in welcome.

No Minister Skelch.

Mage Agassiz cleared her throat. "I was informed that Minister Skelch had arrived. Just a moment, please." She stepped offstage.

People in the audience started to mutter and everyone behind the screen fidgeted, unsure whether they should put down their puppets or not.

"Have you noticed the Minister is always late?" said Stephan.

"You can be late if you're important. Everyone waits for you," said one of the grade nines.

It was true, thought Wil. The Minister was late for the bus to Narcisse. Late for the masquerade ball. Late for the committee meeting...and now...late again.

The voices of the audience were getting louder, punctuated by Mage Quartz's loud laugh.

Mage Agassiz strode out again onto the stage. She clapped her hands, and the voices subsided.

"Minister Skelch has indeed arrived. Apologies for the delay. Would you please join me in welcoming his Excellency, the Honourable Minister Skelch."

Wil stole a glance around the screen at the Minister. Not to be outdone by Mage Agassiz's emerald robes, Minister Skelch was wearing voluminous blue robes lined in gold braid. Drawing out a sheaf of papers from inside his robe, he intoned:

"Today, we re-enact the Narcisse play, a tradition from the time when our beloved Gruffud's was founded in MiddleGate. As we all know, the May shadow play tradition hearkens to the very beginnings of Gruffud's, long before the Persecutions.

"Many of us here today have taken part in the Narcisse Play. I myself remember holding a chorus puppet in a stirring performance of *Wizards Woken* when I was in grade nine...how nervous I was—but enough reminiscences from an old man, for we are here this afternoon to enjoy this year's play: *The Box*, written by Francis Woe—a play that reflects on mysteries, and the limits to what we can and cannot know."

At this, Minister Skelch paused, drew a deep breath and turned back to his papers.

"As you know, we celebrate the emergence of the...the...snakes of Narcisse. This display of herpetological powers can be seen nowhere else in the known world. We celebrate the emergence of —yes, the snakes of Narcisse. This display of herpetological powers can be seen nowhere else—"

Minister Skelch stopped again, apparently searching for his place on the page.

"Ah, yes, here we are...nowhere else in the known world. The world of serpents' shadows is at times more real, more expressive of the human imagination than...than...ah...flesh itself."

Why does he keep losing his place? thought Wil.

"My deepest apologies that I will not," continued Minister Skelch, "be able to stay for this afternoon's performance, as planned. Other, er—" He coughed. "—pressing ministerial duties must be fulfilled."

Sounds like he's trying to hide something, thought Wil.

"I do look forward to attending Saturday evening's performance," said Minister Skelch. He bowed deeply to Mage Agassiz and left the stage quickly.

Despite the terrible dress rehearsal earlier in the day, the play went off without a hitch. The phosphoworm lanterns cast a steady light and no one mixed up the puppets. The singers remembered every cue, and by the end, Mage Terpsy was beaming as much as the phosphoworms.

With the closing of the curtains, thunderous applause burst out. Someone near the front shouted, "Bravo, bravo!"

Members of the choir bowed, the players filed out and bowed, and someone handed Mage Terpsy a magnificent bouquet of orange and blue dragonspot lilies.

Finally, Wil was able to push his way through the crowd to find Aunt Rue, Aunt Violet and Mr. Bertram.

"Have you seen—" Wil started to say.

"Wil, wonderful performance!" exclaimed Aunt Rue.

"One of the best plays I've ever seen," said Mr. Bertram, holding out his arms. "My train got here just in time. Give me a hug, my boy!"

Wil, forgetting about Sophie for a moment, didn't care that Mr. Bertram's tweed jacket was scratchy. The old, familiar smell of mints filled the air.

"What a terrific performance! Where's Sophie, my dear?" asked Aunt Violet, peering at everyone milling about.

"You don't know where she is either?" Wil asked.

# XLV  Secret of Secrets

*Could these have belonged to the Serpent's Chain?*

---

*QUID IN HERBA LATET? SERPENS.*

*NE VOTA NOSTRA NUMQUAM SOLVANT.*

WHAT HIDES IN THE GRASS? A SNAKE!

O, THAT YOUR WISH AND MY WISH NEVER SHALL BREAK.

---

Wil fidgeted in Gruffud's Office, waiting for Aunt Rue, Aunt Violet and Mr. Bertram. The three of them were being interviewed—perhaps interrogated was a better word—by the Firecatchers.

Wil kept glancing at Mage Terpsy, who was sitting directly underneath the portrait of Mage Simone Goldstocking, one of Gruffud's past principals—a severe-looking woman holding a purple plumed pen in one hand and an open book in the other. Mage Terpsy was rocking back and forth, jabbering something about *if only.*

I have to find Sophie, he thought. Everyone just seems to be talking and not doing anything ...but if even the Firecatchers don't know where she is, how will I find her?

Leaving Mage Terpsy to her misery, Wil quietly slipped out of the office without anyone noticing.

Rae Bridgman

Portia and Portius were no help. Despite being made of stone, they too had been reduced to singing lullabies after the Firecatchers finished with them.

What if the same person who kidnapped me has got Sophie— Wil stopped short as an idea popped into his head out of nowhere.

The blue egg.

Adderson had said, *This egg will remain in my office for safe-keeping, until such time as the owner claims it.*

It was an outrageous idea. But things were serious.

———

Mage Adderson's office was along the east wing of Stone Hall; many of the teachers had their offices there. Although the hallway was usually filled with bright sunlight, on this overcast day, it seemed gloomy and deserted. All the doors were closed. Wil padded nervously down the hall to Adderson's office, which was near the end.

What would he do if Adderson were there? He listened at the door, but there was no sound. Then he tried the doorknob. It was locked. He noticed a spiky plant right beside the door. It was a snake plant, he thought with a jolt—just like Mage Radix's plant and like his grandmother's. On a hunch, he bent down.

Hidden underneath the pot was a key...and the key fit the lock perfectly.

Mage Adderson's office was long and narrow, lined on each side with glassed bookcases filled with hundreds of books. It was as neat as any room could be, not a speck of dust anywhere. There was not much room to hide anything.

Wil scoured the floor for any cracks or special knotholes, but there were none.

The sound of footsteps came down the hall and Wil held his breath.

The footsteps stopped; a door opened and shut.

Heaving a sigh of relief, he crept over to Adderson's desk. Unlike the rest of the office, it was piled high with papers, half-open books, and cramped equations and notes on scraps of paper.

He opened the desk drawer.

No blue egg.

He eyed a wooden box sitting on the desk. It was too obvious, but it was the perfect size for holding the blue egg. He tried lifting the box, but

162

it was stuck to the desk. He opened the lid; the box was empty. Perhaps there was a secret compartment. He felt around the edges of the box and found a slight indentation in the wood. He pushed it and there was a clicking sound, like a latch being pulled. "Got it!" he whispered.

He lifted the lid of the box again, and there, nestled inside, was the gleaming blue egg. He picked it up, and carefully put it in the large pocket inside his uniform. He tiptoed out of the office, locked the door, replaced the key and trotted back down the hallway—just in time, for Mage Terpsy was weaving down the hallway.

"Mr. Wychwood," she said. "sorry, sorry state of affairs...if only..."

"I was just handing in an assignment to Mage Tibor," said Wil, his heart pumping so wildly, he thought she would surely hear it. "Mage Tibor asked us to bring it to his office."

Mage Terpsy's blue and green eyes teared. "Oh, such a conscientious boy, imagine thinking about your schoolwork at a time like this."

Embarrassed, Wil hurried off as quickly as his feet would take him. Not only was he stealing blue eggs. Now he was telling lies.

Well, what else could he say? "Oh, Mage Terpsy," he whispered in a high, squeaky voice. "Don't mind me—I was just sneaking into Mage Adderson's office; I really needed the blue egg."

Wil walked back to Half Moon Lane, dodging puddles, past the monument of the Brimstone Snakes in Grunion Square. When I first moved here, he thought, I used to think all the houses were so crooked. But I don't notice it any more. Funny how you get used to something.

—⚬—

Mrs. Oleander was sitting on her front porch reading *The Daily Magezine*. "Shouldn't you be at school?" she asked Wil with a sniff.

"Hello, Mrs. Oleander," said Wil, trying to sound as pleasant as possible, even though Mrs. Oleander hardly ever seemed to have much good to say about anything. "There's no school this afternoon."

Wil was about to ask if she had seen Sophie, but Mrs. Oleander scowled and returned to the newspaper.

All was quiet in the house but for the ticking of the grandfather's clock. Wil called out, "Sophie, you here?"

Cadmus meowed from upstairs somewhere, and Wil ran up the stairs to check Sophie's room. Her room was as it always was—the bed rumpled, school books sitting haphazardly on the desk, and drawings scattered all over the floor and taped to the walls, the ceiling and even the mirror. Cadmus was stretched out on Sophie's bed. He jumped down and rubbed around Wil's legs, purring loudly, until Wil tickled his chin. Wil walked down the hall to his own room, followed by Cadmus. Esme was coiling around a branch from which a dried husk of translucent skin hung.

"So that's why you've been grumpy the last few days, Esme," he said.

When she moulted, Esme's skin peeled back like a sock from a foot. You could hear the crinkling and crackling of the skin; sometimes she looked back at herself—it was like having two snakes attached to each other. And there was always a small snap when the last bit of tail came out.

Wil opened the cage;Esme glided out and coiled around his arm.

Cadmus took one look at Esme and, tail held high, darted from the room.

"Sophie can't have disappeared," Wil said to Esme, as he carried her down to the kitchen. He put Esme in his pocket, and more out of habit than anything else, sat down at the kitchen table beside a plate of ginger cookies. There were crumbs on the table. Perhaps Sophie ate one of the cookies when she came back to get the library book, he thought.

From the corner of one eye, he saw Cadmus's tail disappearing into his uncle's study. He darted from the table.

"Cadmus, what are you doing? Aunt Rue will have a fit."

Wil peeked into the study. Dominating the room was a large oak desk covered with stacks of papers. And sitting on top of the desk, Cadmus.

"Cadmus, go on. You know you're not supposed to be in here."

Cadmus jumped down and a piece of paper fluttered to the floor.

I bet he knows something's happened to Sophie, thought Wil. He bent down and scratched Cadmus behind the ears, and looked into his amber eyes. "It's all right; we'll find her."

Cadmus meowed.

Wil looked around the room. It was as if the room's occupant had just stepped out, and was about to return. Feeling as if he were trespassing, Wil half-expected to turn around and see his uncle standing right in the doorway. He looked back at the desk. Gold-rimmed eyeglasses were sitting on top of a manuscript, which had a gold-leafed letter *S* in the top left-hand corner. None of the words that followed the *S* made any sense.

Wil bent down again to pick up the paper from the floor. It was a letter—written to someone named Bart—about a Narcisse manuscript.

..."umbra nullam umbram facit" *translates as "a shadow has no shadow," or "a shadow casts no shadow." I'm dismayed that we haven't cracked the code yet. The coiling serpents illumination is so vivid. I am certain that it is the key to another gate out—*

The letter ended mid-sentence.

"A gate out?" whispered Wil. He glanced again at the large *S* on the manuscript. "But a gate from where to where?"

Cadmus meowed again and rubbed against the corner of a red leather book, which was poking out underneath one of the piles of paper. Wil pulled the book out. *Forgotten Magic* by Veltanda Brumos.

His heart pounding, he flipped through the pages to the letter *S*. "Serpent's Chain ... Serpent's Chain," he muttered, running his fingers down the pages. "It's got to be here."

He turned another page. There it was—

*The Serpent's Chain was a secret society during the Middle Ages, the origins of which are shrouded in mystery. Little is known about the society, but an organization known as The Chaine of the Serpents is first mentioned in the Black Hand Codex (c. 1356).*

*References to a Serpent Chain Societie occur several times in the seventeen volumes of 'The Golden Circle' by the noted historian, Oligant van Stone Fliegelstopper (1776 – 1866). An undated manuscript originally held in a private collection (its current whereabouts are unknown) and associated with the Serpent's Chain is known by the cryptic name, the* Secret of Secrets *manuscript. Many of the society's members were charged with heresy and immorality, and the society was thereafter forced to disband.*

Wil turned the page to a small engraving of a chalice engraved with symbols in the margin of the book. The caption under the engraving read *The Star Chalice*:

*The Star Chalice is also associated with the Serpent's Chain, and was documented by one Jeremy Wight, Esq., a reputable collector of medieval antiquities in the early 1900s. The drawing in fig. 1 came from his personal papers. The chalice was apparently marked by several symbols (including a serpentine figure), the meanings of which are presently unknown. Sadly, the chalice is reported to have been melted down in aid of the war effort.*

Wil stopped as a small beetle teetered across the page and then he continued reading.

*A round black disc similarly inscribed with some of the markings found on the Star Chalice was also found among Mr. Wight's papers and donated to the Grunwald Museum upon his death in 1955, but it disappeared under mysterious circumstances.*

"Cadmus, what does it all mean?" Wil asked, as he scratched Cadmus behind the ear.

Cadmus rubbed his cold, wet nose against Wil's hand.

Wil reached into the pocket of his jacket, and held the medallion up to the light. It seemed ordinary enough, a dull black except for the coiling serpent, which glinted in the sunlight.

Cadmus pawed at the medallion.

Aunt Violet had gone into some kind of trance after she touched the medallion, and she began to sing *Beware the Serpent's Chain*—there was something else about friendship, but he couldn't remember it all.

He spun the black medallion; the shimmering star appeared. What if this were Jeremy Wight's black disc? If it were, the snake and the star might have secret meanings that only the Serpent's Chain would know. He wondered if the ring belonged to the Serpent's Chain too.

Wil turned back to the letter on the oak desk.

*...serpent illumination is so vivid. I am certain that it is the key to another gate out.*

"Did Sophie read this letter, Cadmus? Where has she gone, do you know?'

Cadmus hissed, jumped down from the table and ran from the room. Wil turned to follow Cadmus, but noticed something moving on the desk out of the corner of his eye.

It was Esme gliding over the manuscript.

"How did you get out of my pocket, Esme?"

He picked her up, but she slipped through his hands and slithered back to the manuscript. Wil stared as she coiled around the strange words and the *S*.

Perhaps Mage Terpsy's *mixusfixus* charm could unscramble the words so they would make some sense. They weren't supposed to practise magic outside Gruffud's...but Sophie's life was more important. Wil took a deep breath and drew a circle counter-clockwise in the air.

"*Mixusfixus.*"

Before he could have said snickety snake, the letter *S* turned into two writhing snake-like creatures.

Esme wound herself around them protectively.

# XLVI  Brimstone Snakes

*An incessant rustling like wind...*

---

*NE TORMENTUM IMMITTAS UT MUSCAM NECES.*
DON'T FIRE A CANNON TO KILL A MOSQUITO.

---

"Those are just like the Brimstone Snakes," whispered Wil. "Maybe that monument is a secret gate and maybe that's where Sophie went. And where would the Brimstone Snakes take someone but to a place with snakes, right Esme? They must take you to Narcisse."

Esme, still coiled around the *S*, looked up at Wil.

"Come on, Esme." He scooped Esme back into his pocket, closed the study door and scribbled a note.

> *Looking for Sophie at Brimstone Snakes*
> *Maybe a secret gate to Narcise their Wil*

Wil hurried along Half Moon Lane and passed Mr. Druce, who lived down the street and worked at Lludd's Bakery. He was carrying several loaves of fresh, steaming bread.

"Hello, Mr. Druce," said Wil.

"Wet day," said Mr. Druce, and he waved a loaf.

By the time Wil got to Grunion Square, the rain clouds had disappeared; the Brimstone Snakes were glistening in the afternoon sun. Steam rose from the metal scales and a double rainbow stretched across the sky above Grunion Square.

Wil ran his hand along the base of the monument, looking for a crack or a secret door. Nothing. He put his ear to one of the snakes, and knocked on it. A deep, dull sound reverberated inside the metal. Then he climbed to the top of one of the snakes, and sat there, shielding his eyes from the sun.

"You be careful," said a voice below. "Those snakes are wet and slippery. You'll get your sash dirty."

Wil looked down. Mrs. Frontino, who lived around the corner on Earbend Street, was peering up at him. Her baby was stretching out her arms, clearly eager to climb the snakes too.

"Yes, Mrs. Frontino," said Wil.

"Not until you're older, Sweetums," said Mrs. Frontino, struggling to hold the wriggling baby. "Let's go home for lunch."

Wil stroked the head of one of the snakes, as *Sweetums* howled for the next two blocks. The snake's large, lifeless eyes seemed to glint.

"Maybe I need a key. Or maybe a password. Mr. Bertram always said, 'Don't fire a cannon to kill a mosquito.' But what have mosquitoes got to do with anything? Or cannons? Maybe if I had a cannon, I could get inside these snakes." Wil hit the side of the snake in frustration, and yelped. The muffled knock resulted in nothing more than scraped knuckles.

"Stupid snake," Wil moaned, feeling silly sitting on top of the monument and talking to himself. His shadow looked like a lumpy crown on top of the snake's head.

He slid back down. Now thoroughly wet, he walked around the base of the monument. There was something shiny underneath one of the large boulders.

Three blue jewels.

And peeping out between two boulders was a book...*A History of Gruffud's*.

Something terrible must have happened to Sophie. Wil looked around to see if there were any other clues and saw smeared chalk lines on another boulder. Blurry letters, almost impossible to read: *u m b r a n u l l a*... What were the words in Cyril Isidor's letter? he thought.

"*Umbra nullam—*" Wil closed his eyes, trying to remember. "*—umbram facit.* That's it! *Umbra nullam umbram facit.*"

Wil climbed back to the top of the Brimstone Snakes. "*Umbra nullam...umbram facit.*" He stumbled over the words, then said them again more loudly. "*Umbra nullam umbram facit.*"

Nothing happened.

But Balbulus's *Magykal Spelling, Grammar and Palaver* always said really powerful incantations had to be said three times.

"*Umbra nullam umbram facit!*" he shouted.

Before he had finished saying the words a third time, the mouth of one of the Brimstone Snakes gaped open. Wil was jerked forward and pulled upside down deep into its belly. He tried to scream...but his scream was swallowed up, his breath snatched away. He felt as if he were being flushed down a spinning whirl of frozen air.

All at once, he tumbled out of the whirl into a pile of dry brush. Dizzy and disoriented, he turned around to see where he had come from. All he saw was a large boulder covered in lichens and near an old oak tree.

He groped inside his pocket. "Esme, you all right?"

Esme's small face peered up at him, her tongue flicking.

He checked his other pocket warily. Miraculously, the blue egg hadn't cracked. He staggered to his feet.

"Mage Tibor was right, Esme. There *is* another gate."

He bent down and picked up something shiny from the ground. Another jewel—unmistakably a blue gem from the Snow King's cloak. Sophie must have come this way.

Wil tried to get his bearings. Feathery leaves were greening the trees, and the air smelled of spring mud. Crows called in the distance, and several sparrows chirped nearby. There was not another soul in sight.

"All these stone trails—we *are* at Narcisse, Esme," he said. "And I remember the boulder and that oak tree. We must be near the second cave."

He found one more jewel stamped into the ground by the heel of a boot. At the second cave, hundreds of slithering snakes writhed across the rocks in frenzied, tangled mating balls. A dense, pulsating ball of snakes slithered up an aspen sapling, and when the writhing ball fell, the snakes splashed on the rocks like water; they swarmed again and rolled away.

There was no one at the second cave—Wil supposed it was getting too late in the day for many visitors—and he was about to walk on when he caught sight of two handkerchiefs on the rocks below near the cave entrance. One was the faded, pink handkerchief he remembered from the school trip last autumn, but the other one was not faded—it looked new.

Wil clambered down the rocks, trying not to twist an ankle or skin his knees. He saw a shiny stone and pounced. Another blue crystal.

"Esme, we must be on the right track," Wil said. He looked around for more jewels; there were only two old bubblegum wrappers. He picked up the new handkerchief and squinted into the dark cave.

He was about to say, *Sophie, are you there*? But what if someone else were in there? he thought. And worse, what if Skelch were in there?

All around him, Wil could hear an incessant rustle—like wind through dry leaves— almost as if the dry grasses and thistles were whispering *SSSophie*.

Wil crawled into the narrow cave on hands and knees through the writhing river of tangled snakes. Rocks scraped his shins and Wil felt his heart pounding. He began to feel ill from the damp, airless smell.

He looked behind; sunlight was pouring in the cave entrance. Then he heard a muffled sound. The hairs on the back of his neck tingled unpleasantly. Crawling slowly, he groped along the cave wall. Now there was a stench of rot—such a revolting smell that he retched. He held the pink handkerchief to his nose.

Suddenly, he was dazzled by the flash of lantern light. He ducked behind a rock ledge, then peered cautiously around the rock. Sophie was huddled on the cave floor near a mound of dead snakes. Her hands were tied behind her back with her sash. Beside her, someone was stuffing live snakes into a pink pillowcase.

Wil grasped the ledge and strained to see who it was. He inched forward, but a small pebble broke off the ledge and fell to the cave floor.

Whoever it was turned at the sound.

171

# XLVII Snake in the Grass

*Umbris nos dedamus.*

---

*NEMO SEMPER POTEST VIVERE. NASCENTES MORIMUR.*

NO ONE LIVES FOREVER.

FROM THE MOMENT OF BEING BORN, WE DIE.

---

It couldn't be—but it was—Miss Heese.

"Mr. Wychwood—we are ssso honoured. Come to rescue Misss Isidor?" A cruel smile crossed her face. She threw the pink pillowcase onto the cave floor. "How gallant of you."

"Miss Heese, what are you doing here?" asked Wil, incredulous, still not believing his eyes.

Miss Heese looked at Wil and her eyes narrowed.

"I thought...I mean—you aren't Minister Skelch," stammered Wil.

"What are you blithering about?" said Miss Heese. "That man hardly knows one end of a sssnake from the other. A more foolish man I've never met. I tried to reason with him that night at the Winterlude Carnival."

"Is that how the Snow King's cloak got ripped?" asked Wil.

Miss Heese sneered, "That SSSnow King businesss went to his head. We merely borrowed the cloak to visit you in the tent, when Massster Meninx so conveniently left. No one knew the difference. The cloak makesss the man—or the king—and people sssee what they want to believe."

Keeping his eyes on Miss Heese, Wil ran over to Sophie. Tears had stained her face, and her robe was torn.

"I was on my way back to school," whispered Sophie, "when I saw someone sitting on top of one of the Brimstone Snakes. It turned out to be Miss Heese. I heard her saying those *umbra* words, only her voice was really strange, and then she disappeared all of sudden."

"I found the blue jewels and the library book...and the words you must have written too," Wil whispered back.

"Clever of you to follow usss here," said Miss Heese, drawing out a pink handkerchief from her pocket and wiping her hands. She threw the handkerchief down. "But now, what *shall* we do with both of you?"

Wil watched several snakes slither out of the pink pillowcase and then stared at the pink handkerchief lying on the cave floor. He pulled the handkerchief from his pocket—it was the very same. He threw it down in disgust, then pulled the blue egg out.

"You let Sophie g-g-go," he said, holding the blue egg above his head, "or you'll be sorry."

"You've come armed, have you, Mr. Wychwood?" said Miss Heese. "A firebird egg. That wouldn't be the one Addersson confissscated, would it? The day that egg rolled into SSStone Hall—" Miss Heese snorted.

"I t-t-told you," said Wil, his voice quavering. "You let us go, or I'm going to throw this."

"Mr. Wychwood, we think not," said Miss Heese. Before Wil could throw the egg, she pointed her finger at him. "*Glacio!*"

Wil's arm froze. The egg slipped from his hand and dropped to the floor. Blue fumes begin to trickle into the air from a small crack in the eggshell.

"Poor Mr. Wychwood. Beware blue eggsss."

Before Wil had a chance to move, Sophie managed to kick some of the dead snakes over the egg to cover it.

Wil thought wildly. "*You* rolled the egg into Stone Hall."

Miss Heese laughed unpleasantly. "No. That egg was in my safekeeping. But Peerssslie stole it one night; then I suppose he couldn't resissst playing a trick. But to businesss." Miss Heese's voice hardened. "I must thank you for bringing the black medallion to usss."

"The black medallion?"

"Yes, the black medallion belongs to the SSSerpent's Chain. We have been sssearching for it for years, not knowing whether it ssstill exisssted. Your ssstupid grandmother refused to relinquish it. You're lucky to be alive, you wretched boy. I've had to bide my time ever sssince Winterlude. The Firecatchers have been sssuspicious and SSSkelch—"

"What do you know about my grandmother?" Wil asked.

Miss Heese seemed to be standing far away. She was looking at him without remorse, her mouth moving, but Wil could not hear the words at first—his mind was spinning.

"...Chain does not take no for an answer, sssilly boy," said Miss Heese. She laughed mirthlessly.

Wil shot a glance at Sophie, who was tilting her head ever so slightly towards the mouth of the cave.

Wil turned back to Miss Heese. I have to keep talking to distract her, he thought. "What are you doing with the snakeskins?"

"You and SSSkelch—he asked the same question. Do you remember the two sssskeletons?"

"That was you and Skelch?" asked Wil.

"Clever boy. You want to know why the sssnakes are ssso valuable? Eternal youth."

Miss Heese smiled at Wil.

Wil, overcome again by the smell of rotting snakes, gagged.

"The sssnakesssskins brew a potion of eternal youth for those who choose to drink it. SSSnakes renew themsssselves—ssso shall we. Join the SSSerpent's Chain, and you will live forever."

"No one lives forever! All of us—we all die!" Wil shouted.

Wil ran headlong at Miss Heese and pushed her backwards. Caught off guard, she fell against the cave wall. Her thick, white glasses shattered on the cave floor, and her dandelion hair caught on a fragment of sharp rock.

Wil gazed in shock at the clump of dandelion hair dangling from the wall.

A wig!

He stared back at Miss Heese, whose hair was black. Heese was a man—a man with spiky, coal-black hair.

Wil's mind raced to the storage room in the basement of the library, and the man who had interrogated him. Of course, it must have been Heese.

Heese's words replayed in his mind. *Your stupid grandmother refused to relinquish it.* At that moment, Wil realized the full horror of Heese's words. Heese must have been the man with the black hair—the same man who ran away from the fire.

"You...killed...my...grandmother." Wil choked on the words and his eyes filled with blind rage. "You killed my grandmother!"

Wil flailed, and the lantern smashed against a rock; the light fizzled out. A streak of light exploded from the black medallion.

"Run, Sophie, run!" Wil shouted.

# XLVIII Escape

*You never know who may be listening.*

---

*ADIUVA!*

HELP!

---

Hands still tied behind her back, Sophie pulled herself to her feet and ran to the mouth of the cave. Her left foot caught in a vine and she stumbled, then gagged over the sour taste in her mouth. She scrambled up the slopes of the gully back to the path, her knee throbbing.

Snakes glided silently out of her way.

The sun flashed in her eyes and she fell over a jutting tree root.

"Oh, ou-ou-ouch!"

Salty tears welled up.

# XLIX  Lunge

*It could always be worse.*

---

*AUT INVENIEMUS VIAM AUT FACIEMUS.*

WE SHALL FIND A WAY OR MAKE ONE.

---

Heese yanked at the chain around Will's neck and snatched the black medallion, but Wil bit Heese's hand hard.

"Ssserpent'sss ssscale!" cursed Heese.

The gold ring scuttled across the cave floor along with the medallion, whose tiny serpent glowed more brightly than ever.

Wil grabbed the ring and the medallion, but Heese kicked his arm. The medallion flew to the other side of the cave. Wil scrambled after it and clambered through the snakes to the entrance of the cave. He tried to throw the medallion as far as he could.

Heese grabbed his arm. "Ssstop!" he shrieked. "You'll lose it, you ssstupid boy!"

Wil managed to fling the medallion a short distance.

With a screech, Heese push Wil aside and crawled after the medallion on his hands and knees. But as if it had a mind of its own, the medallion rolled into a fissure in the rocks. Clawing at the rock with his bare hands, Heese pulled at the medallion, but it remained firmly lodged. Muttering to himself, he kept trying to pry the medallion loose.

Rae Bridgman

"Sssecretsss...return to usss."

Wil pulled himself to his feet. He was shocked at the greed in Heese's eyes. Gone was any recognition that Wil even existed—Heese was so bent on possessing the medallion.

Gasping for breath, Wil whispered, "*Adumbro.*"

Before Wil's eyes, his shadow quivered; pulsing, growing, its edges blurred. The shadow's hands and arms joined its body, and its legs no longer two, but one, stretched out and coiled. The shadow quaked and curled back upon itself.

As if he had separated from himself, and was standing at some great distance, Wil saw Esme stretch her head out from his arm...her mouth agape and hissing. His shadow, no longer the shape of anything recognizably human, swelled—larger and darker. It was the shadow of a snake. A forked tongue darted from its serpent head, and the shadow cut away from Wil's feet without a sound. He concentrated all his thoughts on that shadow, willing it to grow. The shadow of the snake grew larger still , its black more dense than coal.

With a final tug, Heese pulled the medallion out from the crevice. Seemingly unaware of any danger, he held it above his head triumphantly. A moment later, he threw it down with a shriek; it skittered along the ground.

"It burns," he moaned. "It burns."

Then with one great lunge—a moment of shock registered in Heese's face—Wil's shadow swallowed Heese's shadow whole.

The belly of Wil's shadow swelled and bloated, looking like Esme after she had swallowed one of her eggs. Wil staggered, so weighed down that he could hardly put one foot in front of the other. He shivered, and felt a chill cold, colder than anything he'd ever felt before. Moving in slow motion, he bent down to pick up the medallion. Each breath sent sharp pains racking through his body. He clutched the medallion and sank to the ground.

Heese's knees were tight to his chin; his arms coiled tightly around his legs.

Like an egg, thought Wil. It was as if Heese were being held by an invisible straitjacket.

"We reclaim what is rightfully oursss, Wychwood," said Heese, his voice hoarse and barely audible. "I saw the black medallion your firssst day in the library. A black medallion takes care of its owner, but you do

**178**

not know how to use it." Heese opened his mouth wide and laughed, but the laugh was hollow.

Wil felt the hairs on the back of his head tingle. His arms and legs felt numb.

"These things have been sssecret for countlessss generations. You are but a ssstripling of a boy—a clever boy, but hardly a match for the SSSerpent's Chain.

"Ah, the sssun begins to ssset. I will sssoon be free."

At this last sentence, Heese tried to stretch out from his prone position, but pitched to one side. His face hit the dust.

"My grandmother, my grandmother gave me the black medallion." Wil's voice broke.

With a deep groan, Heese rolled onto his back. "It was not hersss to give, Wychwood," he hissed.

Something tugged steadily at Wil's shadow, willing its way out. His shadow strained to hold on; the cold was piercing his lungs.

Heese wheezed, "Perhapsss your fate liesss with usss, Wychwood."

Unable to move his head, Heese turned his eyes toward Wil.

"Yesss, the tasssksss—you will do the black medallion's tasssksss. A black medallion will kill anyone who is not one of usss."

"That's not true," said Wil. But a nagging doubt entered his mind. He tried to push back the doubt and his shadow trembled.

The sun was now almost touching the horizon.

Heese stretched and strained, the fingers of his hands convulsing. Shocked, Wil remembered the dream about the brown snake that had turned into a small human-like creature with furry arms.

Wil's shadow held.

"No...Serpent's Chain," said Wil, his teeth chattering.

"Are you ssso sure?" whispered Heese.

Wil's shadow buckled, and Heese managed to turn his head and look directly at Wil. The pupils of Heese's eyes were small, fixed, and slit-like.

"Live forever," said Heese in a choked voice. "Join usss. You will live forever, boy. Join usss, William Wychwood."

"No—you're wrong. Nothing lives...forever," whispered Wil.

# L Help

*A great shadow passed over her.*

---

*AUXILIUM PROPE EST.*

**HELP IS NIGH.**

---

Sophie hobbled along the path, wincing with each step. Her ankle throbbing, she rested against the stump of an old tree and worked at the sash binding her wrists. With her hands finally free, she leaned on the stump and tried to take another step; her right ankle gave way and she crumpled on the ground.

"Fine, Sophie. Look at you." She reached for a stick and stabbed the ground. "Great help you are."

She drew an outline in the moist earth of a large bird with outstretched wings.

"I wish I had wings like you."

She tried to stand again, but the wrenching pain in her ankle forced her to the ground and she didn't see a great shadow pass over her.

The shadow of a large bird—a raven, perhaps—circled once, then raced back along the path just as the sun was beginning to set.

# LI Lullaby

*...like a thousand snakes lisping a hissing lullaby.*

---

*CUPIDITAS RADIX MALORUM EST.*
**GREED IS THE ROOT OF ALL EVIL.**

---

The tugging on Wil's shadow grew.

Esme, tongue darting, drew herself up high and coiled around Wil's head, staring straight at Heese. Wil felt his shadow grow stronger—but not by his will alone.

It's as if Esme is helping me, he thought.

A hissing sound grew louder and louder in his ears. The sound was comforting, like a thousand snakes lisping a hissing lullaby. The sense of stabbing, bitter cold—of not being able to breathe—vanished, and Wil was awash in what felt like a warm spring breeze.

The lullaby was broken by the sound of footsteps crunching on stone. Wil struggled to open his eyes and saw someone—it was Mr. Bertram—standing over Heese.

Mr. Bertram said a strange thing.

"Rufus, black hair—not red?"

# LII  Empty Pockets

*There are powers at work in this country and beyond.*

---

*CINIS SUMUS ET UMBRA ALBA.*

**WE ARE NOTHING BUT ASHES AND A PALE SHADOW.**

---

Cadmus sat at the head of the table with a snatch of cream, and Esme had a place of honour in the middle of the table; but she seemed not to care that Sophie and Wil were heroes. Esme had curled up inside her small hut, the tip of her tail and snout of her nose just visible.

"You always did make the best snakecake, Aunt Violet," said Mr. Bertram, his face beaming. "Food too fine for angels."

Aunt Violet's cheeks flushed, and she shuffled dishes to make room for a steaming platter of strawberry waffles. "Here, Bartholomew, you must try one of these—my great-grandmother's recipe."

With its familiar high-pitched whistle, *The Daily Magezine* shot down the chimney. A puff of ashes spewed from the fireplace into the living room.

"Let's see if the paper says anything, shall we?" said Aunt Rue.

Before she had even finished her sentence, Sophie and Wil were already scrambling to get the paper.

"Ouch," squealed Sophie, rubbing her arm.

Grinning, Wil held up the newspaper—but there was a large rip slashed through the picture of Miss Heese that filled the front page along with the headline

### BRIMSTONE SNAKES LONG-LOST PORTAL
### SNAKE IN THE GRASS CAPTURED

"Read on, Wil," Mr. Bertram said. "What does it say?"
Wil began to read:

*Two children discovered the Brimstone Snakes monument is a long-lost gate to the caves of Narcisse, and the mystery of who has been behind the murder of the snakes of Narcisse drew to a close last night. Authorities have also at long-last apprehended the notorious rogue known as the Snake in the Grass.*

"Who could have known that Rufus Crookshank was the Snake in the Grass?" said Mr. Bertram. He turned to Aunt Rue with a look of deep sadness.
"It's hard to believe, isn't it, Rue?" he said. "Cyril, Rufus and I—such good friends—and to come to this."
So his uncle, Mr. Bertram and Heese had been friends, thought Wil. Maybe that's what Portia and Portius were talking about. *Three friends— one no longer with us.* Cyril Isidor must be the *one no longer with us.*
"What happened to Miss Heese, I mean, Rufus Crookshank, Mr. Bertram?" asked Wil. "Was he always—"
"Today is a day for celebrating, not rehashing ancient history," said Aunt Rue, in a tone that brooked no discussion.
"So sorry, Rue. You're quite right," said Mr. Bertram, and he tried— unsuccessfully—to smile.
After taking another bite of his waffles, Wil continued reading.

*Minister Skelch of the Secretariat on the Status of Magical Creatures will present Certificates of Bravery in a special ceremony to Sophie Isidor and William Wychwood—*

"Wait until Sygnithia and Sylvain read this!" Sophie interrupted.

*—who were instrumental in the capture of Rufus Crookshank, alias Miss Verena Heese, newly hired this past year as Head Librarian at MiddleGate Library.*

"They don't say anything about you, Mr. Bertram," said Sophie. "But you helped capture him too."

"My part was very small, Sophie," said Mr. Bertram, "hardly worth mentioning. You and Wil were doing very well by yourselves."

At that moment, there was a loud knock at the door.

"Who could that be?" Mr. Bertram asked and he jumped up. "Don't read one word more, Wil. I don't want to miss a thing!"

Mr. Bertram returned moments later with a package the size of a loaf of bread. The names WILLIAM WYCHWOOD and SOPHIE ISIDOR were scrawled in huge letters across the front of it.

"Look what's come for both of you, children," said Mr. Bertram.

"For us?" asked Wil. He took the package and unwrapped the brown paper. Inside was a blue box.

"Open it, open it," said Sophie, bouncing up and down in her chair in excitement.

Wil lifted the lid to the blue box and found a red box inside. "A box inside a box," he said, laughing. "Just like the play."

More and more boxes.

Sophie began to pile the boxes one on top of the other. "Nine, including the tiny white one," she announced.

As Wil lifted the corner of the white box, they heard a low, moaning sound as if wind were escaping from the box. Then Minister Skelch's voice boomed out in mid-air.

*Dear Miss Isidor and Mr. Wychwood:*

*You are hereby notified that you have both been charged with practising magic as minors this past Thursday in contravention of the Division of Magical Misdemeanours and Malpractices By-Law—"Regulation of Magic by Minors," Section 10.2.3, Parts (a) and (b); and in contravention of the Ministry of Magical Education's By-Law—"Regulation of Magic for Educational Purposes," Sections 5 and 6.*

Wil could hardly breathe. He remembered Sophie telling him once that anyone caught practising magic off school grounds would be questioned by the Firecatchers.

"They can't be serious," said Aunt Violet, as her hand fluttered to her throat.

> *Mr. Wychwood is also charged with harbouring a magical creature—namely the snake Esme—without a licence, in contravention of the Secretariat on the Status of Magical Creatures By-Law 73—"Licensure of Magical Creatures—Domestic Provisions," Section 9.1.*

"Does that, does that mean they're going to take Esme away from me?" Wil asked, panic rising in his voice. "It was Esme who saved me. Without her, my shadow would have been too weak. I know it would have been too weak."

"Don't worry, Wil," said Aunt Rue, patting his hand.

"We'll sort this out," said Mr. Bertram at the same time.

Minister Skelch's voice continued,

> *You are hereby notified that the charges against you both in the first instance have been waived, in view of extenuating and life-threatening circumstances. In the second instance, you, Mr. Wychwood, are hereby required to register your responsibility for said creature, Esme, within five working days of receipt of this letter. Upon failure to so register, the Secretariat will be forced to confiscate said creature. We anticipate your co-operation in this matter.*

Sophie, Aunt Rue and Aunt Violet clapped their hands, and Mr. Bertram patted Wil on the back. Wil smiled with vast relief.

> *In due consideration of your bravery and assistance to authorities in apprehending a known criminal, you both shall also be honoured in a special ceremony.*
>
> *Arrangements will be confirmed under separate cover.*

> *Yours sincerely,*
>
> *E. Sibelius Skelch*
> *Minister of the Secretariat on the Status of Magical Creatures*

With these words, the whistling sound diminished, until only the ticking of the grandfather clock could be heard.

"Both of you, congratulations!" said Mr. Bertram. "A special ceremony too. I'll have to get out my best robe for that."

Rae Bridgman

"You can go to the Secretariat tomorrow, Wil, to register Esme," said Aunt Rue. "We certainly don't want her confiscated."

"We'll all go together," said Mr. Bertram. "Now let's hear what else it says in that newspaper. What about Rufus, Wil?"

His heart thumping, Wil picked up the pieces of the newspaper once more and searched for the place where he'd left off.

> *Rufus Crookshank, who always speaks of himself in the plural as "we," was notorious for his trickery. He shed many false names during his travels, and was tagged by authorities as the Snake in the Grass for his genius at disguise and escape. When he wanted to hide, he simply disappeared from the face of the Earth.*

"I told you so!" Sophie jumped up and almost knocked over Cadmus' bowl of cream. "Remember when I said Miss Heese was always saying we?" Wil nodded.

> *He is an elusive "deal-maker" and key figure in the killing raids on the snake population of Narcisse, facilitating the capture and slaughter of thousands of the snakes. When dried and pulverized, their skins are one of the ingredients in a potion promising everlasting youth. Crookshank called himself a middleman.*

"What does middleman mean?" Sophie asked, as she looked over Wil's shoulder at the newspaper.

"It means someone who acts as a go-between or a messenger," said Aunt Rue, and she served a generous dollop of applesauce and sour cream onto Mr. Bertram's plate.

Wil turned back to the newspaper. He was having difficulty keeping the two ripped pieces of the front page together. Miss Heese's eyes were glaring in different directions—it was very distracting.

> *Environmentalists world-wide have been concerned that the snake population was endangered.*
> *In an interview two years ago in the popular magazine, Burning Heart, Crookshank explained, "I broker human desire. We—all of us—have certain requirements, certain needs. I help others do what they wish to do, don't I?"*

**186**

Wil thought about how Miss Heese—or rather, Rufus Crookshank—had argued for the play about the elixir of life. It was hard not to think of Miss Heese as just that—Miss Heese. Rufus Crookshank was someone who had left Wil to starve in the basement of MiddleGate Library, someone who had killed his grandmother—not the person who had helped Wil with his homework and saved him special books. But that was only because Rufus Crookshank had wanted the black medallion, he reminded himself.

"Why are you stopping? What else did Crookshank say?" Sophie jostled Wil's arm, and took the paper from him. She continued reading:

> *"A gift from one to another helps to grease the wheels, so to speak, doesn't it? Is it a bad thing—to help people achieve their dreams? What is the harm in that? Why not be young forever? Surely we are much more than ashes and a shadow."*

"Ashes and a shadow," Wil repeated as he watched Cadmus's tail flicking back and forth. For some reason, the words seemed so bleak.

Mr. Bertram shook his head again. "Ashes and a shadow, yes. But that doesn't lead all of us to desperate acts or to snuffing out life's candle. This is the talk of a madman."

> *After arresting Rufus Crookshank, police emptied his pockets and purse in a pile, and carefully itemized everything.*

"What did they do that for?" asked Sophie.

"To make sure he didn't have any dangerous weapons, I should imagine," said Aunt Violet with a twinkle in her eye. "There's no telling what you'll find in a lady's purse."

"There's a column here with a list of everything in the purse," said Sophie.

"Really?" asked Aunt Violet, her eyes bright with interest. "Well, let's hear."

Sophie started to read the list:

> *2 library cards (in different names)*
> *1 Canadian postage stamp worth 1¢*
> *an American silver dollar dated 1966 (with the image of the Liberty Bell beneath the full moon)*
> *a stamp (issued in the Year of the Snake) worth 55 Canadian cents*

Rae Bridgman

*3 driver's licences*
*passports from 6 countries (all in different names)*
*a black notebook (with the embossed initials RC)*
*a worn map of Canada*
*a Swiss Army knife*
*a gold pen*
*a compass*
*a long clear glass vial (empty) with cork*
*1 pencil*
*an English dictionary (with gilt edges)*
*a sewing kit*
*1 film canister with a dead bee in it*

"A dead what?" asked Wil.
"A dead bee," said Sophie.
"That doesn't make sense," said Wil.
"I know, but that's what it says," said Sophie.

*seven Band-Aids (including one already used)*
*one pair small scissors*
*a creased and stained photograph of a woman stan-*
*ding on a beach*
*a bottle of dried "snake's breath"*
*a bottle of echinacea*
*a bottle of pulverized ginseng*
*a bottle of hand cream (empty)*
*three brushes*
*a train ticket*
*three pink silk handkerchiefs*

"How did all that fit in her—I mean, his—bag?" asked Wil. "Who's the woman in the photograph? And where was the train ticket to?"
"It doesn't say," replied Sophie.
"All so strange," said Aunt Violet. "There must be much more to this than *The Daily Magazine* is letting on."
Sophie turned the page.

*When the inventory was complete, Rufus Crookshank/*
*Verena Heese was conveyed to the local Firecatchers' post.*
*A trial date has yet to be set.*

*Mage Agassiz, Principal of Gruffud's Academy, expressed
her great relief that the Snake in the Grass had been caught,
and has assured authorities she will do everything she can
to assist them in their investigations. "Gruffud's Academy
has always been committed to the highest moral ideals for
our young people," she said.*

*Minister Skelch of the Secretariat on the Status of
Magical Creatures (SSMC) was not available for comment,
but one of his deputy assistants has assured* The Daily
Magezine *that tight security around the Brimstone Snakes
and the Narcisse caves will continue to be enforced.*

*According to one government source, who spoke on
condition of anonymity, the Firecatchers suspect Rufus
Crookshank may be one link in an organization known
as The Serpent's Chain.*

"The Serpent's Chain? What's it say about the Serpent's Chain?"
asked Wil, leaning forward to reclaim the newspaper.

"There's not much more," said Sophie and she reached for a chocolate muffin.

Wil's turned to the last paragraph.

*The official declined further comment other than to say,
"There are powers at work in this country and beyond about
which we have scant knowledge."*

Wil shivered and looked up from the paper before reading the final
sentence.

Aunt Violet, Aunt Rue, and Mr. Bertram all had their heads bent.

Esme's snout was poking out from her hut.

Cadmus stopped licking the cream from his paws.

Sophie's eyes were great dark orbs, her eyeglass frames, purple shot
through with ruby swirls. Her hand was clutching the chocolate muffin
mid-air and her mouth was half-open.

Wil reached for the black medallion and gold ring hanging about his
neck, and began to read the last sentence.

*A secret society dating to the Middle Ages, the Serpent's Chain
was believed by many—*

Wil heard Heese's—no, it was Crookshank's—voice echoing in his mind. *Yesss, the tasssksss, you must do the black medallion's tasssksss. A black medallion will kill anyone who is not one of usss...of usss...of usss.*

What tasks was he talking about? And why had Aunt Violet said in that rasping voice—not her own voice at all—*Beware the Serpent's Chain*?

The Serpent's Chain must not have been destroyed after all. Wil took a shallow breath and started reading the last sentence again, his voice tight.

*A secret society dating to the Middle Ages, the Serpent's Chain was believed by many to have been long vanquished.*

At the word *vanquished*, Cadmus jumped at a bee buzzing around the jar of honey. The tower of boxes swayed and toppled to the floor.

As Sophie and Wil scrambled to pick up all the boxes, Sophie whispered to Wil, "So it's back. The Serpent's Chain is back."

# The End

# Acknowledgements

*Why fear the waking of the garter snakes?*

*The Serpent's Spell* is inspired by the red-sided garter snakes (*Thamnophis sirtalis parietalis*) of Narcisse and Inwood, Manitoba. These non-venomous snakes hibernate in limestone caves over the winter months—although they are not true hibernators, as some mammals are, for reptiles cannot control their own body temperatures. Instead they spend the winter in a state known as *brumation*. Their mass brumation is unique in the world and renowned internationally; they emerge by the thousands each spring and return to their hibernacula (or snake dens) in the autumn.

The support of the Manitoba Arts Council for the writing of this book is gratefully acknowledged. My thanks go to Carol Steer and Elaine Fantham for their help in translating the proverbs at the beginning of each chapter into Latin.